# DYLAN RAMIREZ IS MY FORBIDDEN BOYFRIEND

## RUMORS AND LIES AT EVERMORE HIGH #3

### EMILY LOWRY

Cover Art by
DƯƠNG NHÂN VIA PEXELS

 ELEVENTH AVENUE
PUBLISHING

## A THANK YOU FROM EMILY

I wanted to take a moment to say thank you to my readers —
without you, none of this would be possible.

I truly appreciate every single review, Instagram post and
blog shout-out that you have given me. Every email, message
and kind word from you has brightened my day, every time.
You are the true MVPs!

To my ARC team, thank you for your endless encourage-
ment and incredibly helpful feedback. I value each and every
one of you.

Now, to write my next love story. Stay tuned!

Lots of love always,

XO, Emily

## JORDYN

*G*lass shattered.

The sound was punctuated by a brief silence, then mom started yelling again. When she got really riled up, she loved to throw things. What was it this time?

"Come one, come all, and place your bets!" I put on my best sideshow booth hustler voice and mimed sticking a microphone in my brother's face. "Tell me, young man — what is it that mom just trashed? A vase? The 'good' china that we never use? A photo frame?"

I expected my twin brother, Chase, to laugh. Instead, he paced across his bedroom, looking concerned. It was one of the rare nights he wasn't with his girlfriend Abby, and truthfully, I was thankful to have him by my side. Even if it meant being trapped in his room, which smelled like someone accidentally punctured a can of cheap body spray.

"Going once." I shoved my imaginary microphone closer to his mouth.

He pushed my hand away. "I don't feel like it, J."

"This game is not optional, young man," I said with forced

cheerfulness. "You can either play the game or you can face reality. Of those two options, which would you like?"

He sighed, resigned. "A photo."

"Bold prediction."

"There was a clunk after the glass broke." Chase slouched and rubbed his eyes. "And there wasn't that scattering sound that comes with the vase."

We knew way too much about the sound household objects made when they hit the wall. "I'll accept photo," I said. "But — for the bonus prize — which one?"

"Sixth grade school photo."

"Mine or yours?"

Chase didn't need to answer that. He was the all-star quarterback. He was going places. I was... his sister. As far as my mom was concerned, I'd be lucky to make it to the corner store without doing something that would embarrass the family for generations.

"Shame it'll be mine," I said. "Your sixth-grade picture is horrible."

"It's not that bad."

"It was so bad that, upon seeing your gap-toothed smile, dad sent you to the best orthodontist in the state. You had braces forever. You probably still have them."

Chase glared. As confident and popular as he was, his childhood teeth were still a sore spot — the kind of spot that only an annoying sister could aggravate. He sat next to me on the edge of his unmade bed. His hands gripped his thighs, turning his knuckles white. "Should I go down there?"

"And do what? Put yourself between them and tell them to stop fighting? *Puh-lease.* You're not an after-school special." We had this debate every time. Chase, who saw himself as my protector, wanted to step in. I wanted to step out. If my parents couldn't figure out how to be civilized after twenty years together, they'd never figure it out.

Plus, stepping in just made things worse. Mom got madder. Dad got more distant. They never laid a hand on each other, so nobody was in physical danger. They just loved a good ol' screaming session.

"Why don't they just get a divorce already?" Chase asked.

Another question nobody needed to answer. We both knew why.

My parents took the phrase 'Keeping up with the Joneses' literally. When we went out together, it wasn't a family night, it was a presentation. A way to show the world that we were shiny, untarnished. We were the flag-bearer, the standard by which every family should be measured. Divorce meant admitting their marriage was a pretty lie.

I rested my head on my brother's shoulder. He was seven minutes older than me, seven inches taller and seventy pounds heavier, which made him think he was responsible for me. And for everything I did.

I pretended to hate this, but deep down — like, deep, deep, past the confines of time and space — it was nice to have someone looking out for me. Plus, Chase was the only family member I enjoyed being around. Most of the time. He was still a brother, after all.

Chase's shoulders dropped and he rubbed his eyes again. The gesture made him look more like an overworked office drone than a seventeen-year-old football star. "I shouldn't be leaving you this summer."

So that's why he was so stone-faced about this particular parental bust-up.

The family traits for compassion and sensitivity had all gone to Chase. He probably inherited them from our abuela, our wonderful grandmother back in Puerto Rico. Sweetest woman alive. I still wasn't sure how my mom could be her daughter. Maybe empathy skipped a generation.

"We're seventeen," I said. "Practically adults. Well, I am. You have some serious maturing to do."

Chase rolled his eyes.

I persisted. "Fine. Don't laugh at my hilarious joke. Or was it a joke? You *are* pretty immature."

He shoved me playfully.

"See! SO childish."

He laughed and casually whacked me with a pillow.

But I'd made him laugh.

Good. That was what mattered.

Losing Chase for the summer would suck. But I could never, ever tell him that. Mr. All Star Quarterback needed to focus on the future, not his annoying sister who devoured a box of cereal a day.

Chase was more than Evermore High's star quarterback. He was the best high school QB in the state. He had a bright, shiny scholarship ahead of him, and this summer's football camp would be the perfect kick off to his senior year season.

Six weeks alone with mom and dad? I could handle that.

Downstairs, the front door slammed so hard the house shook. An engine revved and tires squealed out of the driveway.

"Storm's over," I said. It was time to get out of Dodge. "Hailey's party?"

Chase nodded. "Hailey's party."

"We need to grab Dylan on the way?"

"I'll text him."

Dylan Ramirez was my first crush. Past-tense. He was the grade-A hottie all the girls crushed on, and back then, and I was the idiot who momentarily became one of those girls. He was tall, dark and handsome, and came complete with a smirk that said he knew he was gorgeous.

Puh-lease. Soooo predictable. Dylan Ramirez was a total player.

He was also my brother's best friend. They started playing football together before they were potty trained, and by the time they reached high school, they were the perfect quarterback and running back combination. The standout football stars at Evermore High.

And my crush on Dylan? It happened when I was twelve. It was nothing, a stupid schoolgirl fantasy about a boy I'd been friends with since I was a toddler. I was so embarrassed that I reverted to teasing Dylan about everything — and I do mean everything. Once, to justify why I was staring at him during a family dinner, I started making fun of how he held his fork. Later, I tried to tease Chase and Dylan about our moms bathing them together as babies. My mom overheard and corrected me — apparently they bathed all three of us together. She even fished out a photo for evidence.

That was a fun day. Note the sarcasm.

Staring down at the photo of three babies lined up in the bath together, I vowed to lock my silly little crush into the deepest, darkest pit of my existence. Dylan and I were life-long friends, our fate sealed for us when we were just infants. Dylan Ramirez would never like me like *that*. So, I shouldn't like him that way. I pushed my crush far out of my mind, and since that day, Dylan had just been like a second, equally annoying brother to me.

And I was determined: that was all he ever would be.

As an equally annoying brother, he was entitled to certain privileges, such as getting a ride to the year-end bash. Today was the last day of junior year at Evermore High. My best friend, Hailey Danielson, was throwing an epic end-of-year party at her mansion before she jetted off to Europe for the summer.

Ugh.

With Chase and Hailey both gone, who would I have to hang out with this summer?

And more importantly — how was I going to get out of this nightmare of a house?

My phone vibrated, distracting me from my thoughts.

It was a blast from Click, Evermore's anonymous gossip app. Through Click, anyone could write anything about anyone, regardless of whether it was true or not. So, what was on the docket today?

*School's out for summer, but gossip is forever. Word on the street is that our fave couples, Chase and Abby, and Trey and Hailey, will be out of town for most of the summer. Sounds like a golden opportunity to dish the dirt on someone new... so come on, Evermore, cast your vote - who is your new favorite?*

I rolled my eyes, feeling a deep surge of pity for whoever Click decided to follow this summer.

## 2

## DYLAN

The kitchen of Beachbreak Burgers was hotter than a summer afternoon in the Arizona desert. Beef, bacon, and onions sizzled on the griddle, and my t-shirt clung to my body, damp with sweat. At the smell of the food, my stomach grumbled.

It was almost 7pm and I hadn't eaten since noon. My dad, the owner of Beachbreak, had a strict rule: no eating while working. Apparently, it was a huge food safety violation. I didn't argue. There was no point in arguing with dad; he was stubborn as an ox.

The service bell rang.

"Order up!" My older brother, Luis, yelled.

"Order up," I repeated, turning my attention back to funneling fries into baskets.

Luis rang the bell again. "Ashley? Dylan — where is she?"

"Take a wild guess."

Ashley was SUPPOSED to be one of Beachbreak's waitresses. But when the dinner rush hit, she disappeared. She claimed her slow service was because she was chatting with the customers, which was an important part of the Beachbreak experience. However, the only customers she chatted with were her friends from Evermore.

Where was she this time?

I scanned the restaurant, peering through the cheerful families celebrating the first day of summer vacation.

Ashley was plunked at a booth in the back corner, yapping away to her friends. She looked more customer than waitress, and when a balding man asked her for something, she lifted one finger to say 'just a minute,' then turned back to her friends.

Anger boiled in my stomach. I clenched my jaw so tight my teeth hurt. I was a patient guy, but I had no time for people who weren't willing to put in an effort. Especially when my family was paying them to work.

I slung my dishcloth over my shoulder and balanced plates of burgers and fries precariously on my arms. I wasn't the most graceful waiter in the world, but at least when I was serving, your food actually arrived at your table. I whisked the overflowing plates off to table 26, then ducked behind the bar to whip up a waiting order of milk shakes.

As I added vanilla ice cream and caramel syrup to the blender, I peeked into the kitchen.

Dad was on duty at the griddle, wielding a flipper in one hand. He hunched forward, his other hand resting on his lower back. Dad worked harder than anyone I knew. His hunched back was a permanent reminder of the long hours spent slaving at Beachbreak to provide for his wife and three kids. We joked that Beachbreak, the restaurant he'd opened after moving to the USA to start a new life, was like his fourth kid.

Still grinding my teeth, I set the milkshakes on the counter.

Ashley returned and glared at me like I'd done something wrong. "Table 26 didn't order milkshakes. I know they didn't. If you're going to ring the bell and tell me that the order is ready, at least make sure it's the right order, mmkay?"

*Keep calm, Dylan. Keep calm.*

"They're for table 27."

"Table 27 wasn't ready to order."

"Oh. I wonder why they came up to the till to place their order, then?"

"Well maybe if they'd been ready when I was, they wouldn't have had to do that." Ashley sniffed. "So, let me know when there's another order, mmkay? My friends really need me to be there for them."

I looked past her to her friends. They were all smiling and laughing with each other.

"I need you to take over the till so I can get through the backlog of shakes," I struggled to keep my voice calm and in control.

Ashley scrunched her face like the cash register was the most disgusting thing on the planet. "I'm a waitress, not a cashier. It's not really in my job description."

She wasn't joking, but I laughed anyway. How could I not? Taking orders and collecting payment was literally her entire job description.

"What's so funny?" she asked.

Shaking my head, I said, "You're fired."

Her eyes darkened. "Are you kidding? If you fire me, you'll be completely understaffed."

"So literally nothing would change?"

"Ugh. Whatever. You know, I liked you Dylan. I thought you were cool." She untied her apron and threw it at me.

I caught it deftly in one hand and watched as Ashley spun on her heel and marched out of Beachbreak, not even bothering to collect her friends on her way out.

She would not be missed.

I hated firing people. I believed that everyone deserved a chance to show the world what they could do. But if you had that chance and you weren't even willing to put in an effort? That was completely unacceptable. Dad raised me and my siblings to believe that effort was everything. It was the Ramirez way, he said.

In the two minutes it took me to fire Ashley, a line had formed at the register. The milkshakes would have to wait.

"Good evening, welcome to Beachbreak Burgers. Sorry for the wait — what can I get for you?" I took the next three orders before jumping back on milkshake duty. My phone vibrated insistently in my apron pocket, probably messages about Hailey Danielson's end-of-year bash, but there was no time to check right now.

"You look like a hot mess." The voice belonged to my little sister, Sofia. She'd come through the back and was already tying an apron around her neck. "Need a savior?"

"You're late," I said, smiling.

"Probably because I seated a few people who booked the river side tables on my way in. That's right — I was working before I even got to work. Boom." She mimed an explosion with her fist. "Where's Ashley?"

"Fired her."

"About time."

"Are you going to be all right out there? It's packed."

"Pfft. Have you met me?" Just like that, Sofia was off. My sister was shy and insecure with almost everyone outside of our immediate family and her best friends. We joked that Sofia was so ridiculously competent that she could run all of Beachbreak by herself, blindfolded and with her arms tied behind her back. It wasn't really a joke.

I finished mixing milkshakes — two chocolate, two strawberry, and one caramel — delivered them to their tables, then finally checked my phone.

Four new messages. The first was from our school's notorious gossip app, Click.

*School takes a break for the summer, but high school drama doesn't. It starts tonight with Golden Girl's annual rager. 8pm, sharp. Rumor is that Stonewash Sunrise is making an appearance. But don't get too excited, ladies — Trey Carter's taken.*

*And remember — we're going to pick a new fave to follow this summer. Who will it be? Get your votes in.*

I ignored that one. Click was a horrible app that spread life-ruining rumors. My best friend, Chase, had been a victim earlier this year. Click alleged he was a cheater. The lie almost broke up him and his girlfriend, Abby, before they even got started.

The second message was from Chase.

Chase: Yo dude, we're headed to Hailey's now. Need a ride?

The third message was from Jordyn, an hour later.

Jordyn: Please hurry. Abby is eating Chase's face, and at the rate she's going, she'll be done soon. WHOSE FACE WILL ZOMBIE ABBY EAT NEXT? MINE? YOURS? STAY TUNED FOR THE NEXT EPISODE OF: MY BROTHER'S ZOMBIE GIRLFRIEND.

I laughed. Jordyn had a way with words.

Dylan: Stuck at work. Be there in a few hours.

The last message was from Lauren, the girl I was seeing.

Kind of.

It was complicated.

Lauren: Where are you?

The service bell rang. I shoved my phone back in my pocket without replying.

"Give me a hand in the kitchen?" Luis shouted over the sizzle of burgers.

I went into the kitchen, grabbed a knife, and started dicing onions, ignoring the sting in my eyes. "Where's dad?"

Luis wiped the sweat from his brow. "Out back. Needed to sit for a minute."

The unsaid words hung heavy in the air. Dad was looking thinner and paler by the day. Something bigger was wrong — not that he would ever admit it.

"Where's Ashley?" Luis asked.

"Got rid of her."

"Yeah?" Luis flipped a burger. "And who do you have in mind to replace her?"

"A fencepost could probably do the job."

Luis laughed. His face was lined with stress beyond his twenty years. "Maybe, but we're going to need more than that. You decide to get rid of her, you have to find her replacement. That's how it works."

"Not a problem," I said. It was obvious we needed more help.

"Don't you have a party to be at?"

"No time for that," I said. "Some idiot fired the waitress and now we're understaffed."

"We'll survive," Luis replied. "Sofia could run this place by herself. I'm probably just getting in her way. You worry about Beachbreak later. Go out and have fun."

I glanced around the bustling kitchen. Orders were stacked along the pass. We were so far behind that the finish line wasn't in sight. "I'll get you through the backlog first."

"Good man." Luis clapped me on the shoulder. "But you have fun after."

"Will do," I said.

The party could wait.

## 3

## JORDYN

*a* million twinkling fairy lights hung from the pergola in Hailey's backyard. Clusters of silver and black balloons lined the yard's perimeter. In one corner, oversized speakers flanked a small stage. In the other, tiki torches circled the pool, which was filled with floating unicorns. And the hot tub? State of the art, complete with its own light show.

Hailey had a reputation for being extra — one of the many reasons I loved her.

A hired helper wheeled cases of soda on a dolly. One good thing about Click, the app that everyone loves to hate? It made everyone think twice about drinking. Get drunk, do something stupid, and it would be splashed across Click the next morning. Especially if you were popular. I was hyper aware that though I wasn't Chase, if I did anything too crazy, it would affect him. And his future. No way was I taking that risk.

Hailey slipped through the party, smiling and greeting everyone, the perfect hostess. She was dazzling in her black bandage minidress, her gold hair falling in perfect curls. She smiled at the man wheeling the cases of soda, tipped him, then instructed him to put them in the corner.

I loved Hailey, but I hated standing next to her. While she looked like she belonged on a red carpet, I was wearing cutoff Levi's and Chucks, looking much more suited to a country music video.

But why would I bother dressing up? Who was there to impress?

Pete Landry? Evermore's backup quarterback had been obsessing over me since forever. If I wore a garbage bag he would've told me it was a bold and beautiful choice, a brilliant critique on the disposability of modern fashion. Dylan liked to tease me about Pete. He said I looked like I'd rather be getting a cavity filled than hanging out with my sort-of-but-not-really boyfriend.

Pete was nice. That was enough, wasn't it?

Hailey's boyfriend, the notorious Trey Carter, casually strolled through the yard, guitar case by his side. He appraised the stage area. "It's not exactly Prohibition."

"And you're not exactly a star," Hailey said, grinning.

"Yet." Trey smirked. He was the perfect example of a boy who was not-just-nice. Evermore's bad boy turned local music star was smoking hot, dark and broody, but simultaneously willing to jump in front of a train for my best friend. Whenever Trey was around, Hailey got all giggly and flustered.

Had I ever felt like that with Pete?

*Don't open that door, Jordyn.*

Trey set down his guitar case, lifted Hailey off her feet, and kissed her.

"All that for getting you such a small stage?" Hailey said, raising her eyebrows.

Trey waved the idea away. "Nah, I just like that dress thingy."

"Bandage dress," Hailey corrected him. Her new nose stud sparkled under the fairy lights.

Meanwhile, I was busy being invisible.

Before Trey could pick her up again, I roughed my way between them. "HI TREY!"

Trey ruffled my hair like I was six years old. "Hi Jordie."

"Jord-yn." I scowled, adjusted my hair, and glared at Hailey. "Your boyfriend thinks I'm your pet dog."

Hailey rolled her eyes. "Oh, come on, don't pretend you spent any time doing your hair."

"Nothing wrong with being a pet dog," Trey added. "You know I love b—"

"TREY!" Hailey cut him off with a squeal, and smacked his shoulder.

He grinned devilishly. "Gotta go, Jordie. More stuff to unload."

Hailey acted offended, but her puppy dog eyes followed Trey as he went to unload his van. His band, Stonewash Sunrise, were taking center stage at tonight's bash.

"Your boyfriend's a tool," I said.

She couldn't wrench her gaze away from Trey. "You know you love him."

"He's a slight improvement on Adam, I'll give you that. But only slightly." That wasn't true, and we both knew it. Trey was a tremendous improvement on Adam. Yes, he was sarcastic and rebellious, but he legitimately wanted what was best for Hailey. That was what mattered.

"So," Hailey said, still watching the boys at the van, "DeAndre is still single—"

"And I'm not."

"You and Pete are official?"

"I didn't say that."

"So you're single."

"I didn't say that either."

"Has he even kissed you?"

"That's not the point."

"So, no."

"I think he's too nice to try—"

"So you're single."

Steam whistled out of my ears. "No, Hailey. Absolutely not. No, no, no, with a capital N-O. No matchmaking tonight."

The last thing I needed right now was some disastrous set up with another boy I had no feelings for. My parents were acting like children, Chase and Hailey were both gone for the summer, and I was on the job hunt. I had no time for boys, my priority was to figure out a way to get out of my house.

"Fine, I won't play Cupid," Hailey said, pouting slightly. "But you have to have fun tonight. Or if that's too hard, at least be civil to my cheer friends."

"I promise nothing."

## 4

## JORDYN

*C*loying perfume suffocated me, a product of the gaggle of cheerleaders in miniskirts. Somehow, I found myself among them, studying them, trying to fit in, like that researcher who went and lived with the gorillas.

Madison Albright, my brother's ex-girlfriend, held court, telling a mind-numbing story about her stupid hair extensions. How could a story about hair be taking soooo long? And why did everybody else actually seem to care? After the thirteenth complaint about her hairdresser, I sighed.

A little too loud, apparently, as Madison glared at me. "Am I boring you, Chase's sister?"

*Oh, so much.*

I gave Madison a thin-lipped smile. "Not at all, please continue. I'm on the edge of my seat."

Madi narrowed her cat-like eyes, flipped her glossy dark hair, and continued, completely unruffled.

Beside me, Lauren Cowley checked her phone for the millionth time and stamped a pink stiletto in frustration. It sank into the lawn, and when she tried to pull it out, her shoe came off. "Ugh. Grass is just the worst. And where is Dylan already? Like, I told him to be here like two hours ago."

So, he hadn't texted her. Chase wouldn't have been surprised. He said Dylan wasn't really into Lauren, and was having a hard time getting that information through to her. He might not have texted Lauren, but he texted me. He was staying late at work.

Not that I was going to tell her.

Pettiness, thy name is Jordyn Jones.

Lauren crouched and yanked her stiletto out of the grass. "Chase's sister? Do you, like, know where he is?"

"You're the one dating him," I replied, my voice flat.

Lauren went pink, then white, then pink and white all over. "We're not dating. We're… uh… well, it's casual. If you must know. It was a mutual decision."

Madison waved her hand dismissively. "As if you want to be casual with him."

World, stop the presses. For the first time in my life, I was on the same page as my least favorite person. Casual? Lauren was so not casual. She literally Photoshopped him into her Click profile picture. Even then, it was a well-known fact that Dylan Ramirez never got serious with girls. He dated them because it was expected for a star football player to date a cheerleader, but a long-term relationship? True love? Definitely not his style.

I mean, I figured it out and stopped crushing on him. Why couldn't Lauren get it?

"So, like, you don't know where he is?" Lauren tilted her head back as she spoke, literally putting her nose in the air. Like she was better than me. "Chase is his best friend."

"Observant, aren't you?"

"And you're Chase's sister."

"Two for two, Lauren."

"So, can you, like, ask Chase where Dylan is?"

What was I, her personal assistant? I gestured to the pool, where my brother was lying on a lawn chair, his arm around Abby's shoulders. They were attached to each other's faces, as usual. As much as I liked Abby, dealing with their constant making out was as fun as an algebra exam. "You ask him," I said.

"But why can't you?" Lauren tugged at a lock of her shiny blonde hair, genuinely confused.

Ugh. Why did she want to see Dylan so bad? He literally never talked about her.

"I smell food," I said. I stepped away from the cheer squad and went over to my new best friend: the food table. There were six different kinds of pizza.

*One of each, thanks.*

"Jordyn?" Pete Landry stepped in line beside me. He smiled nervously.

I folded a slice of Hawaiian in half and stuffed it in my mouth. "QB2," I mumbled through my mouthful of pizza. A piece of pineapple fell from my mouth and caught on my shirt. I plucked it from the fabric and shoved it back where it belonged.

"Are you having a fun time at this party?"

Oh, Pete. He spoke like he was an awkward dad trying to pretend he was cool.

Slice of pizza still hanging from my mouth, I threw my arms open, gesturing at the yard of sloppy high schoolers making out, dancing, and splashing in the pool. "Best night of my life. The glittering highlight of my existence."

"That's good," Pete said sincerely. "I'm glad you're having a good time."

Why did I even bother trying?

Stonewash Sunrise finished their set and EDM music started blaring through the yard. Hailey was on the dance-floor with Trey, her arms wrapped around his neck. I guess she needed to get all the time she could with him before her trip.

Chase and Abby were still playing tongue twister by the pool. Chase would be gone soon, too.

And me? Little ol' Jordyn Jones was soon to be both jobless and friendless for the summer.

I spun away from Pete.

Time to find something to hit.

## 5

# DYLAN

*I* scaled the back gate to Hailey's party, jumped, and landed softly on the grass next to a discarded red solo cup. I almost didn't have the energy to get back to my feet. The Beachbreak rush didn't slow until 10pm, so I stayed and helped out for hours after my shift was supposed to end. Even then, Luis practically had to force me out the door.

I had five texts from Lauren I hadn't replied to.

Music blared, the bass vibrating in rhythm with my headache. I wanted to go home, crawl under a heavy blanket, and pass out. But I promised Chase and Jordyn I would make an appearance. Even if it was brief.

Taking a deep breath, I officially entered the party.

Chase and Abby were on the dance floor next to Trey and Hailey. I skimmed the crowd for Lauren, but there was no sign of her. Probably for the best. Conversations with her usually left me feeling like I'd just sat through the inanest reality TV show in existence.

"Mine!" The shout came from the pool area.

Jordyn.

She dove and bumped the ball in the air. A guy I didn't

recognize got underneath and set the ball up in the air. Jordyn, already recovered from her dive, took flight. Water cascaded from her body as she launched, scowling, and spiked the ball so hard that she left a handprint in the material. The volleyball slammed down with the ferocity of a comet, and Jordyn pumped her fist in the air.

I approached the pool and casually applauded. "Not bad for someone who hates team sports."

Jordyn pulled her long blonde hair to the side and wrung it out. "Fashionably late, burger boy?"

"I'm a fashion icon."

"Screw your fashion and get in the pool," Jordyn said.

"Why? Need some help?"

Jordyn laughed derisively, her navy eyes flashing. "No, but *they* do."

"Teams look even to me."

"Not in skill level."

You would think that in a set of twins, the ultra-talented quarterback would be the more competitive of the two. You'd be wrong. Despite despising team sports, Jordyn was the most competitive person I'd ever met.

I wanted to play.

But I was supposed to be looking for Lauren. I turned away from the volleyball game and eventually spotted her among a cluster of overdressed cheerleaders. They were examining Madison's hair for some bizarre reason, preening through it like monkeys looking for fleas.

BOINK.

A volleyball bounced off the back of my head.

I spun.

The volleyball landed in the pool next to Jordyn. She casually tossed it in the air and hammered it again.

Right at my face.

I ducked, deflecting it with my forehead.

"You should try catching the ball, aren't you meant to be good at that?" Jordyn said. Her eyes were wide and innocent, her hands on her hips.

"So that's how it is?"

"That's how it is."

I kicked off my shoes and tossed my phone onto a lawn chair. Then, without warning, I cannonballed into the pool.

Jordyn dove out of the way.

I landed beside her, grabbed her in a headlock, and dunked her as she squealed for mercy.

She surfaced, sputtering and glaring. Before she could grab the volleyball, I tipped it out of reach and drifted lazily underneath the net to join the other team, high fiving my new teammates along the way.

"New rules," I said. "We're playing until Jordyn cries."

Jordyn's laugh carried across the party. "Just out of curiosity, will that burger joint pay for your nose job after I spike the ball in your face?"

"You better hope not," I said. "Breaking my nose is the only way you're going to be prettier than me."

Jordyn threw back her head and laughed. "Game on, Ramirez."

"Game on, Jones."

## 6

## JORDYN

*O*nce Lauren and the other cheerleaders decided they wanted to play, volleyball got decidedly less fun. They crowded the pool, splashing and giggling while pretending they didn't know the rules. At one point, Lauren literally caught the ball and threw it back over the net. And when someone spiked the ball? She shrieked and curled up against Dylan, pressing her face into his chest. Anything to get close to him, apparently.

Pete was worse. He insisted on being on my team, and every time he could, he bumped the ball to me. Even when it made no sense. He'd set me up for a spike even if I was in the back row, balancing on one foot, and sputtering for breath. Then, when I couldn't hit the impossible shot he set up, he'd tell me it was okay, he didn't care about winning as long as we were having fun.

Puh-lease. If winning didn't matter, why keep score?

I admit — I may have snapped. I may have said something like "That attitude is why you're a backup and Chase is a starter."

I might have done that.

I climbed out of the pool. Playing any longer was pointless. You couldn't take a half-step without bumping into someone, and the boys were playing with kid gloves. Couldn't risk one of the cheerleaders getting injured. Or worse — getting their perfectly styled hair wet.

The volleyball casually floated from side to side, occasionally catching someone unawares and bouncing off their head.

Dylan stood in the center of the action, cocky as ever. He was, by far, the most muscular guy in the pool. His skin glistened in the moonlight. He shook his dark, shaggy hair, sending rivulets of water flying. Lauren squealed, and he grabbed her playfully, shaking water all over her as she swatted at him.

"Ew, Dylan!" she shrieked.

Dylan laughed, his brown eyes sparkling.

I gritted my teeth. I couldn't believe I had ever had a stupid crush on stupid Dylan Ramirez. Yes, he was hot. But he sure did know it.

Pete followed me like a lost puppy. "Where are you going? Do you need anything?"

Lauren, still in the pool, watched me, a giant grin on her face and one hand twirling through Dylan's dark, wavy hair. "Giving up, Chase's sister?"

I ignored both of them, grabbed a fluffy white towel, and wrapped it around my body.

Pete's wet footsteps smacked on the pool deck. "Can I help?"

"Not unless you can get people to stop referring to me as 'Chase's sister'," I said. "Does anyone even know what my name is?"

"I know what your name is," Pete said.

"My hero."

He took my hand in his. Not in the way two lovers hold

hands, but in the way that a grandpa would hold his grand-daughter's hand before explaining some profound life truth. "Do you want me to talk to them for you? I'm a quarterback. They'll listen to me."

I resisted the urge to shudder, and pulled my hand away. Somehow, despite all the time we spent together, the way Pete held my hand felt gross. Alien. Almost inappropriate. "That'll make it a thousand times worse," I said. "It's fine. I'll just be Chase's sister to everyone forever. And if you'll excuse me, I gotta go change."

"Oh. Do you want me to wait outside the change room for you?"

I wanted him to leave me alone. I wanted everyone to leave me alone. But what was the polite way to say that?

"I think I'm going to head out," I said.

Pete pouted. "Do you want a ride?"

"It's fine."

"Are you sure?" He looked at me like I was a lost child. "I can give you—"

"Pete. It's okay. I'm a big girl."

He bit his lower lip. "I'd just feel better if I knew you got home—"

"It. Is. Fine." I spun away before he continued to protest. He was trying to be nice, trying to do the right thing. But in doing so, he was treating me like a child. Like I couldn't function without him around. And it was so, so, SO frustrating. If I wanted to go home, I would go home. I didn't need someone to walk me to my door and tuck me into bed. Just let me live my life.

I plucked my way through the crowd inside Hailey's house, making my way up the stairs and towards her bedroom. It was a well-known fact that upstairs was off-limits to everyone.

Everyone except me.

I found the key to her bedroom buried in a plant pot in the upstairs hallway, unlocked her door, and let myself into her beautiful pastel-hued haven of a bedroom. I finished drying off, then changed. My cell phone was sitting on her desk, the blue indicator light flashing. A message.

From Click, of course.

The subject line? 'Decision made.'

So. What poor soul was Click going to harass this summer?

I opened the message.

It was directed to me.

*Congrats, Jordyn Jones. You're our new fave for the summer. What big secret is Chase's twin sister hiding? We're going to have fun finding out...*

## 7

# JORDYN

*E*very framed photo in our house was a lie, but the one hanging in the kitchen was the worst offender. Mom and Dad wore matching red sweaters, their smiles plastered on like they were doing an infomercial for teeth whitening. Chase and I sat in front of them, our legs crossed, wearing the same fake smiles. If you looked closely, you could see the concealer on my cheek hiding a cut I'd acquired from trying to jump my bike over a car. I didn't even get the front tire off the ground.

There were more photos like that scattered throughout the house. Fake smiles for a fake happy family. The only time Mom and Dad actually looked happy in photos were the photos from when they were kids. See, they had been best friends since first grade. And they stayed best friends up until they got married, at which point everything soured.

I blamed love. They had a perfectly good thing going until they gave into their more primitive instincts. Falling in love with a friend was the stupidest thing you could do, as far as I was concerned. Friendship lasted forever; love lasted an argument.

I resisted the urge to smash the picture — that was more of a Mom move — and scrounged through the cupboards like I was a hungry racoon. Cooking was out of the question. I couldn't even boil an egg.

I found a box of Cinnamon Toast Crunch stuffed away behind the "healthy" cereal and set it on the counter before turning my attention to the coffee machine. As I waited for my caffeine fix to percolate, I opened my email on my phone. Five more job rejections. Score! A new record! There was no one better at getting rejected from jobs than Jordyn Jones. Four of the rejections were form letters, the fifth cited my lack of customer experience. Apparently, I wasn't qualified to stand behind a cash register in a mall.

Chase entered the kitchen, saw the look on my face, and winced. "Bad news?"

I cleared my throat and read the most recent rejection. "Dear Jordyn Jones. Thank you for your interest in the cashier position at Everending Toys. Unfortunately, we require that all new hires have at least one year of retail experience. We would like to invite you to apply again in the future. Go screw yourself, Everending Toys."

Chase snatched my phone and rolled his eyes. "Sincerely, Everending Toys."

"Same thing," I said, stealing my phone back. I looked at my brother seriously. "Do you think I could learn how to operate a cash register and stock shelves?"

He smirked. "Do you want an honest answer?"

"Do you want your coffee in a mug or on your face?" I snarled, slamming two coffee cups on the counter and sloshing scalding liquid into each. "Can't get a job without experience. Can't get experience without a job."

The ceiling creaked. Mom or Dad had gotten out of bed.

"How long until the next argument?" I asked.

Chase adjusted the picture on the wall until it was straight again. "Are you sure you're going to be okay here?"

"I will be if I can find a way to get out of this stupid house," I said. I filled two cereal bowls to the brim with sugary goodness and poured milk on top. "It'll be tougher to escape without you and Hailey around. I was hoping I could get a job. You know, build a social life that isn't reliant on being Chase Jones's sister."

"I don't have to leave," Chase said. "I can—"

"No, you can't," I snapped. I shoveled a spoonful of cereal into my mouth and chewed furiously. Why was I so grumpy? Because I'd spent most of my morning trying to figure out why Click would be interested in me. The message from Click was also suspicious — it wasn't a full blast to every user. Instead, it came directly to me. Sent anonymously, of course.

Would I find out who was behind it, or was this another one of Click's mysteries that wouldn't be solved? I didn't know. Admittedly, I wasn't much good at solving mysteries.

"It's okay, J," Chase said. He had already wolfed down his cereal and was now slurping coffee extra loudly, like a disgusting caveman. "It's okay for things to be hard — and for you to admit it. If you want, I can get someone to look out for you and—"

"Are you joking?" I had never wanted to slap my brother so hard in my life. I imagined his head as a volleyball and dreamed of spiking it onto hot summer asphalt. Someone to look after me? Like I was a little child instead of a seventeen-year-old woman? It was the single most patronizing thing I'd ever heard. Even if his heart was in the right place, I was not a charity case. "You did not seriously suggest—"

"I'm just saying—"

"No," Glaring, I stood, grabbed my coffee cup, and stormed to the door.

"Where are you going?" Chase shouted.

"Who cares?"

"You're in your pajamas."

"I say again — who cares?"

As I left, I slammed the door twice.

## 8

## DYLAN

*I* checked the order slip twice. A double cheese, garden-style, whole wheat bun. I threw two patties with melted cheddar on a toasted bun, then topped it with sliced tomato, crushed avocado, red onion, and a squirt of Ranch dressing. I wrapped the burger in foil, shoved it in a brown paper bag, and brought it to the front. A woman with a bob cut snatched the bag from my hands without saying thank you and hurried out of the restaurant.

Sofia stood at the till and took orders, blowing a stray strand of hair from her face. The line of waiting customers was so long that the last three people were standing outside in the sun. Sofia didn't complain. She never complained.

She finished taking the order, plucked the receipt, and handed it to me. "Burn two, drag 'em through Wisconsin, garden-style and hog-style, yellow paint on both, two white cows, and put it all on wheels."

I nodded. Two burgers, both with cheese, one with tomato, avocado, onion, and ranch, the other with an extra sausage patty and three strips of bacon. Both with mustard. Two vanilla milkshakes. Everything to-go.

I hurried to the back.

Luis had already thrown two beef patties and a sausage patty on the grill. "How's the line?"

"Out the door and around the building," I said.

"Good." Sweat trickled down his brow. His face was pinched. "You hear about Dad?"

"Not a word."

Luis pressed on the sausage patty with his spatula. "Doc says he slipped a disc in his back. Says he needs to take it easy for three or four weeks. Maybe more. I think we need to give him as much time as we can."

"Agreed." I hustled to the ice cream machine, turned the handle, and let vanilla flow into a plastic cup. Then I added some milk and a few shots of syrup. "You think we can manage this?"

Luis had only turned 20 a few months ago. He put in twelve-hour days at Beachbreak, had done since leaving school, but managing the entire restaurant? By himself?

"We can make it work if you stop firing people," Luis said, smiling.

"Yeah?"

"We gotta. Dad needs the time off. Non-negotiable. I told him he's taking the entire summer. Told him he needs to enjoy himself for once instead of slaving away in a restaurant. Rest up his back then go on vacation somewhere."

"What'd he say to that?"

"He said that there's some big superhero movie coming to Evermore that's going to be shooting in the fall. He wants Beachbreak to try and win the catering contract. He didn't get to say much more before mom cut him off."

That sounded about right. Dad wasn't the best at taking care of himself, but Mom would make sure he took time off. No matter what. "All right. I'm here for you, Luis, whatever you need."

Family always came first. I would bust my gut bussing tables 80 hours a week all summer if it meant Dad got to take some time off. He'd spent his life working for us so we could enjoy life, now it was our turn to work for him.

"Gracias," Luis said.

## 9

## DYLAN

*S*hort-staffed and exhausted, we made it through the lunch rush. There was a peaceful three-hour window in the late afternoon, just enough time for Sofia to clean the tables while Luis and I prepped for the dinner rush. Fortunately, we wouldn't be short-staffed in the evening, as we had another waitress and chef on schedule to help out.

I was taking inventory when the door opened.

"You're supposed to be at camp working on your arm, Jones," I said.

Chase rubbed his hands together greedily. "Couldn't leave town without swinging by Beachbreak."

"Hi Chones!" Sofia piped up. She paused for a moment, her face reddening. "I mean Jase. I mean Jones. Chase."

"Hi, Sofia. How was the rush?" Chase asked.

"Nothing I couldn't handle." Sofia smiled, then continued wiping down tables. It was painfully obvious she had a schoolgirl crush on Chase. Not that she would ever admit it. I teased her about it from time to time, but it was nothing to worry about. There an understanding between best friends — the sister was always off-limits. Not that Chase would've been interested, anyway.

Chase's expression was creased with worry.

"You all right, dude?" I asked.

"Can you take five?"

"Luis—"

"Get out of here," my brother yelled from the kitchen. "Take ten. We'll need all hands on deck tonight."

I hung up my apron. "Let's go to the river. Need to get off my feet."

The late afternoon sun reflected off the river. A cool breeze came off the water, pulling the heat and sweat away from my body. I took off my shoes and plunged my feet in the water, sighing in relief as the cold river lapped around my ankles.

"So, what's up?" I asked.

Chase stared into the distance. "Something's going on with J."

"Something?"

"She's acting weird."

"Weirder than usual?"

"Weirder than usual," Chase said. "She's picking fights. With everyone."

"Doesn't sound that weird."

Chase shook his head. His navy eyes were uncharacteristically stormy, which made him look more like his twin sister than usual. "It's different this time. You know this summer will be the longest we've been apart in our entire lives? I worry about her, man. I worry that if someone doesn't keep an eye on her and get her out of the house, she'll go crazy. She'll do something crazy."

I buried my feet in the sand beneath the water. The voices of people chatting and laughing carried from the Riverwalk.

"I want to help," I said. "But Dad's out of commission for

the summer. And we're short-staffed. You know I care about J, and I'll do the best I can to get her out of the house, but man, this is going to be a tough summer. I don't want to make any promises I can't keep."

Chase rested his arms on his knees. "My parents are going to drive her nuts. I just wish there was a way to get her out of the house. Hailey left for Europe earlier today and with both of us gone, Jordyn doesn't have anywhere to go. And you know how she is — if she's roaming around town, she's gonna start some—"

"What about Beachbreak?" I asked.

Chase chuckled grimly. "I don't think she's going to hang out in a burger joint all day."

"I meant what if she works at Beachbreak? She's smart. Works hard. And we desperately need the help. We hire her, it gets her a job, gets her out of the house, and…"

"And you can keep an eye on her."

I winced. I didn't like the idea that I was supposed to keep an eye on her. Jordyn? She could take care of herself. But I knew her parents. I knew how important it was for her — and for Chase — to get out of the house. That's why he spent so much time focusing on football. He loved the game, sure, but I think he loved getting away from his house even more.

Plus, if Jordyn found out I was supposed to be keeping an eye on her, she might remove both of my eyes.

"I can't promise anything," I said. "But I can get her in for an interview. The rest is up to her."

"Thanks, dude. When I get back from camp, we'll all head up to the cabin and you can tell me all about how she broke you. Seriously. Don't let her push you around too much."

I laughed. "I'm an immovable object, man. Jordyn's never gonna break me."

## 10

# JORDYN

*I* shoved a spoonful of frozen yogurt in my mouth and closed my eyes, savoring the sweetness. Peak's Frozen Yogurt was best enjoyed on a summer day. It was also the best way to stave off the oncoming darkness that a month with no one but my parents was sure to bring.

There was an art to making a good cup of frozen yogurt. You needed to pick two complimentary flavors, then scoop on toppings that would amplify those flavors. For this cup, I'd selected birthday cake and black forest cake, topped with cheese cake bits and cherries. Each bite made my head spin into that perfect kind of dizzy that came with a sugar rush.

Froyo in hand, I wandered down Main Street.

Evermore's Main Street had a distinctly '50s vibe. The street lamps were vintage, cars weren't allowed, and the boardwalk was made of old brick. In the summer, buskers and bands played for the crowd. From one end to the other, you could find everything from a man juggling flaming chainsaws to a dancing violinist playing Disney tunes. And let's not forget the smells! Baked pretzels, cinnamon sugar churros, popcorn, and cotton candy all mingled sweetly together. Imagine an endless old-timey carnival and you have a great idea about what Main Street looked like in the summer.

I loved it as a kid, but I loved it even more as an adult. It was cool for a lot of my classmates at Evermore to hate on Main Street, but honestly, they were idiots. Main Street was the perfect escape. Where else could you find a bench, enjoy the sun, and watch a troupe of actors perform an improvised version of Romeo and Juliet? It didn't have the dangerous charm of that underground night club Hailey was always talking about, but I liked it just the same.

My phone vibrated, rudely interrupting my afternoon.

Two messages. The first was a blast from Click.

"Oh, joy," I muttered. The blast featured a photo of Chase. He was dipping into Beachbreak Burgers and looking around suspiciously. Weird. He was supposed to be on the first bus out of town this morning. The caption on the blast was rather innocent — especially for Click. It read:

*QB1 stopping by Beachbreak to get one last burger before heading out of town. Come back soon, Chase. Summer won't be the same without you and Abby devouring each other.*

I snickered. This might have been the first time in my life that I agreed with Click. I briefly wondered who sent the blast, then dismissed the thought. The app was built on being anonymous. Even if I wanted to figure out who was behind it, I couldn't.

The second message was from Dylan.

Dylan: It's dead right now. Come to Beachbreak. Entertain me.

Hmm… a message from Dylan mere moments after a Click blast showing Chase at Beachbreak. Very suspicious. Very suspicious, indeed. I replied.

Jordyn: I'm very busy. And super important. If you want to see me, you'll have to talk to my receptionist.

Dylan: See you soon.

Jordyn: What's in it for me?

Dylan: The pleasure of my company?

Jordyn: Funny. But what do I actually get?

Dylan: It's a surprise.

Jordyn: The last time you told me you had a surprise for me, you put a bucket of water on top of my bedroom door, told me the surprise was on my bed, then laughed as I got soaked. So excuse me for not believing you.

Dylan: See you soon.

Jordyn: Shut it, burger boy.

Ugh. Chase had probably done something stupid like ask Dylan to look out for me all summer. Watch out for Jordyn, he'd say, she's not strong enough on her own. Make sure she doesn't burn the whole town down. Really dangerous, that girl.

Whatever.

Beachbreak was only a few blocks away… and yes, I'll admit, there was part of me that was very curious if there was a surprise or not.

I'd just have to watch for traps along the way.

## 11

## DYLAN

"You better be sure about this. She screws up, it's on you." Luis gestured in my direction with the spatula. He flipped a burger and threw it on a bun.

"I'm sure," I said. I didn't feel nearly as sure as I sounded. We were desperate for another waitress, and Jordyn was a hard worker. But, part of customer service was the ability to bite your tongue — which was not Jordyn's strong suit. I dreaded the day she snarked the wrong customer and got put on blast on social media.

The door to Beachbreak swung open. Jordyn entered. She wore cut off shorts and flip-flops, her hair pulled back in a messy ponytail. There was a brown stain on her white t-shirt from the frozen yogurt she was eating. I had the distinct feeling her disheveled appearance was the result of a painstakingly calculated attempt to annoy her mother whenever she went back home. There was nothing Jordyn liked more than getting under someone's skin.

"Hey Dyleeeeee!" Her voice was high-pitched and breathy, a perfect imitation of Lauren.

Sofia, who was busy rolling cutlery, burst out laughing.

"Oh my goodness, like how do you even volleyball? Like I don't want it to hit me? Like oh my goodness will you save me from the scary volleyball? Ugh I just can't even?" The impression was uncanny.

I tried to keep a straight face. "Welcome to Beachbreak, can I take your order?"

Jordyn licked off her spoon and scanned the menu, deliberately looking as dumb as she possibly could. "Um, like, do you have, like, um, like I really feel like a light lasagna, and maybe pair it with, like, a milkshake without ice cream or milk? Can you do that for me Dyleeeee?"

Sofia clapped a hand over her mouth to restrain her giggles.

I punched in Jordyn's usual order. "Sounds like you want a Mexiburger, white hot, and a basket of Cajun fries. Cherry vanilla milkshake, or was Peak's enough sugar for one sitting?"

Jordyn touched a hand to her chest, impressed. "And on my hundredth visit, Ramirez finally gets my order right."

"Don't count chickens," I said, "there's still time for me to screw it up."

Jordyn grabbed one of the kids' menus, a tin of crayons, and started coloring. "You should get a new menu. With a new maze. I've done this one a hundred times."

I passed the order slip to Luis. "Make us a new maze and I'll get it done up."

"Can you imagine? Jordyn Jones — maze designer. Just kidding. I'm not qualified for that, either."

"So, the job hunt…"

Jordyn gave a double thumbs down. "Even the entry level jobs want someone with experience. Also, how much do I owe you for the food?"

She tried to pass me a twenty, but I refused to take it. "You're a Jones. The Joneses don't pay at Beachbreak."

"That's a stupid rule."

"My restaurant, my rules."

Jordyn rolled her eyes. "Someone's bossy."

"Correct," I said, laughing. "I could get used to this. I feel powerful."

"Nice apron, Betty Crocker."

"This apron enhances my natural masculinity." I flexed.

The flicker of a smile passed on Jordyn's lips.

"But. Back to your job hunt. I think I can help you out," I said. "Beachbreak needs a waitress. It's minimum wage, but you get a cut of the tips. Have to be willing to work evenings and weekends. That might be hard for someone who's very busy and super important."

Jordyn stopped coloring and eyed me suspiciously. "Did Chase put you up to this?"

I took a deep drink from my water bottle. I wasn't thirsty, but I needed to stall for time. Jordyn was the type of person that would instinctively rebel against whatever you told her to do — even if it was in her best interest. If she found out Chase was involved, she'd run screaming out of Beachbreak.

Lying was the smart thing to do.

But I didn't have it in me. Not with Jordyn.

I swallowed and nodded. "He stopped by. Said something about you wanting to burn the world down if you had to spend the summer locked up with your parents."

"Thought so." Jordyn stood.

"But — we desperately need the help."

Jordyn narrowed her eyes. "Don't lie to me, Ramirez."

"I fired a waitress last night... and Dad's out for the summer."

Her expression softened. "His back?"

"Slipped a disc. Doctor wants him to rest and take it easy for a few weeks. We're trying to manage without him all summer. To do that, Luis'll need me in the kitchen, not bussing tables." I bit my lip. "Look — if you don't want to get involved because Chase came and talked to me, I get it, Jones. I do. But we do need someone. You'd be helping us out big time."

Jordyn looked around. At what, I wasn't really sure. She pressed her lips together, grimaced, then the grimace broke and she smiled. "How about this? I help you out with your waitress situation, and you help me out with my little Click problem."

"Click problem?"

"Someone sent me an anonymous message saying they were going to uncover all of my secrets — of which I don't have any. But I'd still like to know who's tailing me."

I shrugged. "Seems more like a job for Abby, but if you're desperate, I'll help you out."

"Good. Then I guess I can accept the job."

"Whoa." I held up my hands. "You don't have the job yet. You still have to interview. I can get you in the door, but I can't just give you the job."

She rolled her eyes. "Fine. Who do I interview with? You? Luis?"

My lips curled upward like a cartoon villain. "Not exactly."

## 12

## JORDYN

*J*'d never been in the back office at Beachbreak before. A grey computer hummed, the monitor flickering. A schedule was tacked to a corkboard. And, on a small desk in the corner, a fan oscillated, the ribbons trapped in its housing whipping in the air.

Sofia sat behind the desk, tapping a pen to her lips as she examined me.

"And is this what you'd normally wear to a job interview?" Sofia asked. Her playful demeanor was gone. She looked like she should be interviewing college grads for internships at a Fortune 500. When had the shy little Ramirez girl grown into a full-on girlboss powerhouse?

Dylan snickered. He leaned against the wall, his muscular arms folded, amusement dancing in his eyes.

"I'm sorry?" I said. "No one told me there was going to be a job interview. In fact, someone — who shall remain nameless — told me I would be doing them a favor if I were to accept the position."

I shot a glare at Dylan for emphasis.

He tried very hard to hide his smirk.

"I see," Sofia said. She cleared her throat. "I'm going to ask you a series of questions related to waitressing. If you answer these questions to my satisfaction, you may get to experience the joys of working at Beachbreak. Should you fail, you will be banned from the premises, effective immediately."

"You're not serious."

"Does this look like a game to you, Ms. Jones?" Sofia's expression was serious.

She was joking, wasn't she?

"A customer bites into their burger. Unfortunately, due to an error in the kitchen, the burger is undercooked. They complain. They want to send it back. What do you do?"

"Get them a new one, don't charge them for the burger."

"Good," Sofia said. "That concludes the waitressing part of the interview."

Dylan nearly choked. "What? You said you had a bunch of questions to ask."

"And I do," Sofia replied calmly. "Part of being a good waitress is making sure someone has the right personality. I need to know that Jordyn Jones can roll with the punches. So, I'm moving onto the personality portion of the interview."

Great. I was *super* excited about that.

"You've known my brother a long time," Sofia said. "Would you please tell me the most embarrassing story you—"

"That's bull—"

Sofia glared at Dylan. "Luis."

The door swung open. Luis was standing on the other side, clearly listening.

"Dylan has proved problematic. Would you please escort him out of the office?"

Grinning, Luis tugged at Dylan's shirt. Dylan may have

been the big, muscular running back for the football team, but Luis had been a linebacker during his Evermore days.

"I'm not going—"

That was the last thing Dylan said before the door closed with him on the other side.

Sofia could barely contain her laughter, her eyes mischievous. "As I was saying, Jord— Ms. Jones. If you could please enlighten me as to my brother's most embarrassing story, that would be excellent. Preferably one that could be used for, oh, I don't know, blackmail?"

I cracked a grin. "Oh, I've got a good one."

## 13

## DYLAN

*T*he laughter coming from inside the manager's office was unnerving. Sofia didn't know Jordyn that well, but judging from the shrieks and howls, they were already best friends. Jordyn had that effect on people. When you were around Jordyn, you got to be yourself. There was no pretension.

Assuming she liked you. If she didn't like you… well, that was a different story.

The two of them were inside trading their favorite stories. Which ones would Jordyn pick? The time I repeatedly stalled my car in the high school parking lot in front of a bus full of cheerleaders? The infamous pantsing in seventh grade? The torn shorts at the water park?

Eventually, the laughter subsided, and the door opened.

Sofia came out first. "I like her. Seems like she'll be a good fit. And oh, I was wondering if you wanted to go to the water park — provided you're still allowed inside?"

"I'm going to kill her."

I burst into the office.

"Jones!"

Where was she? I checked behind the door.

Nothing.

The closet.

Nothing.

Under the desk.

Nothing.

That's when I noticed — the window was open.

I poked my head outside.

Jordyn was standing a safe distance away, a huge grin on her face. "Guess what? I got the job."

"I can still fire you," I said.

"Oh but I don't think you will."

"Try me."

Jordyn winked and walked off, her voice trailing behind her. "Too bad, Ramirez. You're stuck with me now."

I watched her walk away, my forced frown losing a battle against an easy smile. There were worse things in life than being stuck with Jordyn Jones all summer. At least I'd be working with a friend. A friend who drove me crazy, but a friend nonetheless. Plus, I figured she'd look cute in her new uniform.

*Wait, what?*

I'd known Jordyn Jones forever. I thought of her as the girl who spent her entire childhood with scabby knees. The girl with juice stained sweaters and long blond pigtails who dominated on the monkey bars at recess. The girl with a habit of tapping her foot incessantly when she was bored in class. The girl who loved food so much she could beat Chase and I in any eating competition.

But the girl who was cute? No way.

Not Jordyn.

She was my buddy.

My childhood pal.
Another sister to me.
*...Right?*

## 14

# JORDYN

The booth wheezed as I sat. It was a sleepy Monday afternoon, my first shift at Beachbreak, and the restaurant was empty. Dylan told me Mondays were usually the slowest, then things picked up as the week went on. Perfect for training.

I placed a stack of flashcards on the table and opened a menu. It was my job to know what we were serving inside and out. I needed to know what ingredients were in any recipe, what substitutions were possible, and how everything was cooked. I needed to know what could and couldn't be made gluten-free and what our best vegetarian options were.

This morning, Sofia had taught me Beachbreak's process for taking orders. It was as straight-forward as I imagined it would be, and within a half-hour, I had most of the internal systems figured out. Turned out Jordyn Jones could learn how to do basic customer service work even without a year of experience. Take that, Everending Toys.

A bell chimed as the door opened, and in walked the two people I wanted to see least in the world: my parents. They wore golf slacks and held hands.

Gross.

Dad cleared his throat and smiled at me. "Are you going to take our order, or what?"

"I'm studying," I said. "Sofia can help you."

"We don't want Sofia's help," Dad said. "We're here to support you."

Ah yes. Support by interruption and obligation. Just what you want from your parents. There was no point in arguing — any argument would take longer to get through than it would to just shut up and take their order. Besides, they'd spent their entire lives oblivious to the needs of their children, it's not like they would start paying attention now.

I made my way behind the till and put on my best customer service smile. "Welcome to Beachbreak Burgers, how may I help you?"

Mom appraised my outfit. "It is so nice to know that you can clean yourself up when you want to. And don't you feel better being all squeaky clean?"

I kept my stupid smile plastered on my face. That was mom in a nutshell — if you tried to improve yourself, she'd give you an insult in the form of a compliment. It's like she wanted me to become a better person, but she also wanted me to be slightly insecure about being a better person.

"We'll take two burgers, river style, fries on the side of one. And two chocolate shakes." Dad handed me his credit card.

I processed the transaction, told them to take a seat, then brought the order slip to Luis and Dylan, who were prepping food in the kitchen.

"It's for my parents," I said. "So, fair warning — if it's not cooked perfectly, my mom WILL ask to see the manager."

Luis laughed. "Lucky for you, I'm the greatest cook alive."

Dylan rolled his eyes. "Come on, Jones, I'll help you with the shakes."

I grabbed a steel cup, put it beneath the ice cream machine, and pulled the lever. My parents were the only customers in Beachbreak at the moment, and, as usual, they were having a 'conversation' that was really an argument. At least in public they had the decency to whisper instead of yell and shout.

Unfortunately, even the whir of the ice cream machine wasn't enough to drown them out. I heard my name twice, but with no context. Were they proud of me? Angry at me? Waiting to disown me?

Who knew?

A familiar sense of dread creeped over me, a storm cloud on a sunny day. It felt like a bony hand was reaching inside my stomach.

To fend off the anxiety, I practiced my breathing exercises. A deep breath in through the nose, hold for a count of five, then exhale through the mouth.

"Jones. JONES."

Ice cream slopped over the side of the metal cup.

I swore. "Sorry. I'll clean it."

Dylan handed me a paper towel. "All good. Happens to the best of us."

"Does it?" Anyone with a basic level of intelligence could avoid overfilling a steel cup. I risked a glance over my shoulder. My parents were watching. My mom shook her head and sighed, disappointed. Her daughter wasn't even cut out to work as a waitress.

I vigorously scrubbed the excess ice cream from my fingers and washed my hands in the sink while Dylan finished the shakes. He brought them out to my parents, greeting them cheerfully.

I dried my hands. The good news was that my parents would only show up at my place of employment once. It was a token gesture of support, nothing more. Only now, they saw me screw up. You could bet my mom would tell everyone that HILARIOUS story at every dinner party she had for the rest of her life.

That Jordyn is so silly. She can't even make a milkshake. It's lucky that her amazing brother was there to get her that job or they probably wouldn't have hired her. How could twins be so different?

A few minutes later, Luis slid over two plates. I set them on a tray and brought them out to my parents.

Mom looked concerned. "Did the milkshake machine malfunction?"

"It got stuck," I lied. It was better than telling her that no, the machine didn't malfunction. The only thing that malfunctioned was her daughter's brain.

"Oh, of course it did, sweetie."

I forced a smile. "Enjoy. I have to get back to work."

I returned to my place behind the counter, actively trying to find tasks that would keep me as far away from my parents as possible. Once no one was within earshot, they started arguing again, trading barbs between bites. If you didn't know them well, you wouldn't be able to tell. They'd mastered the art of looking like a happy couple while actually being miserable.

Maybe that was the secret my anonymous Click stalker would try to uncover. And if they did, would that even be a bad thing? If people knew how unhappy my parents were, then we could stop living this ridiculous lie.

"You need a break?" Dylan asked quietly.

"Can't show any weakness," I said.

"Got it." Dylan gently put his hand on my arm. His touch made me jump. What was wrong with me?

Get your head in the game, Jordyn.

"Mom tells me they never used to argue," I said. "She said when they met, they were just friends, and they never

54

argued. I don't know if I believe her not. But if she's telling the truth, that's just more proof that love ruins everything — especially friendships."

"Such a cynic, Jones."

"No," I said, "just a realist."

## 15

# DYLAN

*J*ordyn handled the dinner rush like she'd been waitressing her entire life. She ran at light-speed, her blonde ponytail bobbing behind her. She made customers laugh, knew almost everything about the menu, and bounced around to help wherever she could. Even Sofia, the golden standard for employees, was impressed. With Jordyn on our side for the summer, it felt like we might actually make things work, even without Dad.

I turned the deadbolt and flicked off the neon 'OPEN' sign. My feet were sore and my eyes were heavy, but we'd finished another shift.

Jordyn swept the floor, expertly maneuvering her broom to gather a handful of stray fries and sesame seeds. "So, boss, how'd I do?"

"Handled it like a pro," I said.

"As if there were any doubts." She finished sweeping and poured the dirt into the garbage. She adjusted her ponytail. "Aren't you supposed to be at a party with your precious Lauren?"

"Whatever, Jones." There was a party tonight, and I told

Lauren I'd consider making an appearance. But with my energy at an all-time low, I didn't feel like going home, showering, getting dressed, and going out again. Not when I could just go home and sleep. "Shouldn't you be at that same party? Or wait — did Pete not invite you?"

Jordyn's eyes narrowed.

I laughed. "So he didn't invite you. Maybe he's not as into you as you think he is."

Jordyn scoffed. "Oh, Pete is SO into me. He's way more into me than Lauren's into you. He's practically building shrines for me."

"And that's what you want? A guy who builds shrines for you? A guy who bails you out during a game of volleyball?" I smirked. When you knew someone as long as I'd known Jordyn, you knew exactly what you needed to say to get under her skin.

"EXCUSE ME? BAILED ME OUT?" Jordyn put her hand on her hip. "All he did was make me look bad. I was playing brilliantly before he got in my way. But that's nothing compared to Lauren. Oh, please don't let the volleyball hit me! Oh, please, I'm so scared! Oh, please, can we talk about my hair extensions?"

And now she was getting under my skin.

"Better Lauren than Pete," I snapped.

"Hardly. Pete's harmless. Lauren's actively annoying."

"Only to you."

Jordyn raised an eyebrow. "Oh, so that's the kind of girl Dylan Ramirez wants? A useless one so he can feel super strong and special?"

"Better than some wimp who worships the ground you walk on."

"Pfft. Pete and I are a hundred times the couple you and Lauren are."

I was pretty sure neither Pete and Jordyn nor Lauren and

I were actually classified as real couples, but I would not let Jordyn think I was backing down.

I crossed my arms. "Prove it."

We weren't yelling at each other, but we weren't keeping quiet either. Sofia and Luis snickered in the back office.

"And how do I prove it? Throw a poll on Click?" Jordyn asked. "Maybe I should ask my anonymous admirer what they think?"

"Like you could win a popularity contest, Jones," I said. "Carnival's in town this weekend. I'm sure there's a bunch of games we can play. So why don't we make it a double date? Play some games together? See which couple is superior?"

I sounded cocky, but guilt gnawed at my stomach as I spoke. I'd taken Lauren to two school dances, sure, but I'd never taken her on an actual date before — and here I was, suggesting our first date be at the carnival, with Pete and Jordyn.

What was I doing? What was I trying to prove?

I wasn't sure anymore.

Jordyn threw back her head and laughed. "You realize these games will require some kind of skill, right? And you want Lauren on your side? Sure, I'll go on your stupid double date. It's your funeral."

I extended my hand. "May the best couple win."

She shook. "Don't worry — we will."

## 16

## JORDYN

*T*he scrambler spun in the night sky, a mesmerizing twister of lights, shrieks, and pumping rock music. The scent of cotton candy and deep-fried everything filled the air. It was a warm, early June evening, and it felt like everyone in Evermore was out at the annual carnival. For most of the people here, the carnival was a place of laughter and fun.

For me?

It was the backdrop for a blood-thirsty competition. Me and Pete against Dylan and Lauren. No-holds-barred, winner-takes-all. And I would win.

I dragged Pete through the crowd, lowering my shoulder and bowling through anyone who wasn't quick enough to get out of my way.

"This is nice." Pete started the conversation in his usual mundane fashion.

"Yes." I pulled him faster. We had games to win.

"Thanks for inviting me, Jordyn."

"Sure."

His face was so earnest I felt a pang of guilt.

I shook it off.

Pete was nice. And I was here with Pete. On a double date. Perfectly normal. And certainly nothing to feel bad about. "Come on, we have to meet Dylan and Lauren at the midway."

When we arrived, our opponents were already there, their hands in each other's back pockets with what was, in my opinion, a calculated move to look like the better couple. Two could play at that game. I hurled Pete's arm around my shoulder and put my hand around his waist. Then, wearing my most cheerful smile, I approached the couple I would soon destroy.

"Dylan, Lauren, so great that we could all get out to do this!" I said, mustering as much false cheer as possible.

I shot a beaming smile in Lauren's direction, and she blinked back in confusion.

"Uh, sure. Dylan said you, like, arranged this for everyone."

From Lauren's perspective, this may have been a little random — it was definitely the first time I had voluntarily hung out with her. I changed the pace of the conversation. "Don't you love the carnival?"

"Isn't it, like, for kids?" Lauren said, looking around with thinly veiled horror. She was overdressed, yet again, in tight white jeans, a baby pink halter top, and stacked wedge heels. Next to her, I looked like a five-year-old in my striped shirt and denim overalls. But never mind that. Tonight wasn't about fashion. It was about winning.

I gritted my teeth, but kept smiling. "It's fun for all ages."

"Ok-ayyy."

Dylan flashed me a cocky smile. "You feeling okay, Jones? You look a little nervous. I guess Chase's killer instinct doesn't run in the family, huh?"

I raised my eyebrow. "Did you even play in the last game

of the season, Ramirez, or were you too busy being a Band-Aid?"

Annoyance flickered on Dylan's face.

Good.

I was in his head.

Dylan removed his hand from Lauren's back pocket and clapped once. "So. Should we start?"

I eyed him evenly. "Let the games begin."

"Who picks?"

"Me."

I dragged our quartet to a classic carnival game. There were horribly painted clowns with wide-open mouths. Inside their mouths was a target. All you had to do was shoot water into the clown's mouth until it filled a bar. Fill the bar first, the bell rings, you win.

Pete sat on one side of me, Dylan on the other.

The carnival barker stood on a platform, his red and white striped shirt hanging loosely from his skinny frame. He stroked his goatee and tugged his earring. "On your marks, get set, GO."

I blasted my stupid clown in his stupid mouth, willing the water to go as fast as possible. It took me a breath to find the target, but once I did, I narrowed my eyes and locked on. Nothing and no one would distract me from scoring an early victory for Team Jordyn. Out of the corner of my eye, I saw Dylan make a weird movement, but I ignored him.

There was no way I wasn't winning.

DING DING DING!

The bell rang before my bar was half-full. The winner was…

Lauren?

How in the—

I spun.

Lauren's bar was full, but Dylan's was empty.

And his water gun was pointing at her clown.

He grinned. "Part of being a good couple is team—"

His sentence dissolved into sputters as I blasted him in the face with my water gun. He ducked, and before the carnival barker had the chance to cut off my water, a blast of spray soaked Lauren. Probably ruined her hair.

She shrieked.

The carnival barker yelled.

"You're a sore loser, Jones," Dylan sputtered.

"The games have just begun," I said.

We wandered through the midway to the sound of Lauren incessantly complaining that she was wet, she was cold, and she didn't feel like carrying the small stuffed animal she'd won. At one point, she vaguely suggested throwing it in the trash.

It appalled me. That stuffed turtle was the first trophy in our competition. Who would throw a trophy in the trash? I would've built a shrine to it. And every time Ramirez came over, I would make him look at the shrine with me. Maybe make him bow, too. Or kneel.

The growl of motors roared above the crowd. We'd made it to the end of the midway and arrived at a small Go-Kart track. It was a simple figure eight with stacks of tires for walls. It didn't look particularly safe, but the go-karts didn't look like they could go fast, either.

Dylan grinned wickedly. "I think we've found our next game."

# DYLAN

"*I* don't want to drive a stupid go-kart," Lauren said. Her lower lip trembled.

I resisted the urge to roll my eyes. Lauren was obsessed with the idea that we should all be mature adults, but right now, she was acting like a spoiled toddler. To her, the only proper date was a candlelight dinner at Romano's. She'd wear a dress, I'd wear a collared shirt. We'd discuss politics or history or art. In almost every way, Lauren was the anti-Jordyn.

While Lauren was complaining about being forced to have fun, Jordyn curled her fingers around the collar of Pete's shirt and brought his face so close to hers that their foreheads touched. They were close enough to kiss. I felt a twinge.

Probably just protectiveness.

They weren't kissing, anyway. Instead, it looked like Jordyn was giving poor Pete very detailed instructions on how to drive a go-kart.

"Just tell him gas is on the right and get a move on," I said.

We made our way to the front of the line. There were

four go-karts on the track. Jordyn took the one on the outside, Pete and I took the ones in the middle, and Lauren took the one on the inside of the track. Rust ate through the metal frame of my go-kart. The pedals were loose, the seat belt torn in two places. How did this thing still run?

A bored-looking man stood on the tires near the start line. "Racers, start your engines." He said the words with all the enthusiasm of someone reading the phone book. "On your marks. Get set. Go."

The go-karts lurched forward.

Or at least, Jordyn's did.

Pete drove to the side, smashing his kart into mine, forcing me to swerve to the left — which conveniently blocked Lauren from going anywhere. In fact, the only person to make it around the first corner of the track was Jordyn herself.

"Teamwork makes the dream work, Ramirez!" Jordyn cackled.

"Cheater!"

With one hand on the steering wheel, Jordyn cruised around the track. She pretended to look for a ref. "No flags on the play, Ramirez."

I swore. "Pete. Move."

"Sorry, dude."

I gunned my engine. My tires squealed, metal shrieked, and my kart finally pulled free from Pete's intentional traffic jam. Could I catch Jones?

SMACK.

Jordyn zoomed past, swiping me on the back of the head as she did so. Her cackle was more maniacal than a witch riding a broomstick on Halloween. "Gas is on the right, burger boy!"

Growling, I hit the gas.

Jones would pay for this.

I pulled around the first curve, willing my car to go faster.

Jordyn slowed briefly, then looked behind her, saw I was coming up quickly, squealed, and smashed the gas pedal. She was laughing so hard she was crying. No one on the planet — not even Chase — had as much fun winning as Jordyn did.

She finished her last lap, pulled to the side, and immediately leaped out of her kart — much to the protests of the carnival barker.

Pete and Lauren still hadn't moved.

I pulled up beside Jordyn, unclicked my harness, and scrambled after her.

She was quick.

But I was quicker.

I reached her just as she was about to climb over the wall of tires.

"Wait, Dylan, no—"

Too late, Jones.

I put my head down and tackled her. I didn't hit her the way I would hit someone in a football game, obviously. Instead, I lowered my shoulder, wrapped my arms around her legs, and lifted her off her feet.

But I couldn't stop going forward.

Too much momentum.

We were going to crash into the wall of tires.

I quickly rolled to the side, positioning my body between her and the tires.

BOOM.

We broke through the wall of rubber, tires tumbling over and rolling away.

Still half-tackling, half-protecting Jordyn, I stumbled and fell on my back into the dirt. Jordyn fell on top of me, her forehead thudding against my chest and knocking the wind from my lungs. I kept my arms wrapped around her, holding her close until I was sure we were safe.

## JORDYN

*D*ylan's arms wrapped around me, my hands on his chest, which was... hard? Were those MUSCLES? When did Dylan Ramirez get actual muscles? For just a split second, I forgot myself, and let my hands stay against his solid chest.

The dust settled.

I scrambled off Dylan as quickly as I could and rolled onto my back. There was dirt on my face, on my hands, in my hair. But who cared? I'd won. "And it's all tied up."

Pete and Lauren stood at the now broken wall of tires. Pete had the good grace to look concerned. Lauren? She looked absolutely furious. If a glare could start a fire, I'd already be ash.

I got to my feet and dusted myself off, feigning nonchalance. "Let the games continue."

And they did.

Dylan and Lauren scored back-to-back wins with ring toss and basketball. Pete and I responded by earning three consecutive victories: target shooting, bank-a-ball, and down the clown. Dylan redeemed himself by knocking three metal milk bottles off a platform three times in a row. He also earned a giant stuffed bulldog, which he offered to Lauren.

"I don't want this," she said, sniffing. "It's for kids. Duh."

I rolled my eyes. She whined more than anyone I'd ever met.

Dylan looked exhausted. "Then what do you want—"

"Give it to a kid," Lauren snapped.

Enough was enough.

I stuck out my arms. "I'm a kid. Give it to me."

Dylan looked at me skeptically. "You want a—"

"Gimme."

Holding back a laugh, he tossed me the bulldog. It was almost as big as me.

Lauren rolled her eyes. "Are you going to name it, too?"

"His name is Samuel Danielson," I said.

"That's, like, super weird." Lauren waved her hand dismissively.

Dylan laughed. "Chase's middle name, Hailey's last name. Smooth, Jones."

"You know it."

I carried Samuel Danielson awkwardly on my back while we continued through the carnival. The night was winding down, the crowds somehow both dispersing and getting more chaotic. We'd run out of games to play, but we were all tied up.

As far as I was concerned, that was unacceptable.

"Does anyone see any games we haven't played?" I asked. "See anything up there, Samuel?"

"Ugh, it's a stuffed animal," Lauren said.

I pretended to pout. "Don't you listen to her, Samuel. You're a real dog."

"You're such a kid."

"You're such a kid," I said, doing my best high-pitched Lauren imitation.

"What about that one?" Pete asked, conveniently cutting through the tension. Samuel and I spun to see what he was pointing at.

There was a small tent with pink and white stripes. Flickering pink light bulbs lined the canvas, and a big heart with a neon arrow stood out front. The arrow pointed to the entrance of the tent, over which hung a sign.

Love Match.

## 19

## DYLAN

*E*verything was pink inside the Love Match tent. The floor, the walls, the lights. It was like someone spilled Pepto Bismol everywhere and didn't bother to clean. There were two couches and two tables. Flashcards sat on the table, pink markers next to them.

I held the curtain open for Lauren, Jordyn, Samuel Danielson, and Pete.

"Helloooooo," Jordyn called. "We are here to be matched!"

A few notes played on an unseen piano, then a woman emerged from the back. She had a giant mole painted on her cheek and platinum blonde hair. A wig, probably. She wore the same dress as Ms. Piggy, and her nametag read "Love Doctor."

"Hello, lovers," she purred. She whisked around the room and subtly dragged her finger along my shoulder as she stepped behind me. "Are you here to find your true match? Your true love?"

"I'm here to win," Jordyn blurted. She crossed her arms. As the Love Doctor neared her, Jordyn shifted away uncomfortably.

"There are no winners in love, I'm afraid," the Love Doctor said. She examined Jordyn closely. "Especially for the unfortunates who walk with hearts in their eyes and songs in their hearts. It'll all be dashed like a ship on the cliffs. Unless you visit the Love Doctor and find your true match. Then, your song will sing, and you will have your happily ever after."

She turned from Jordyn, who pretended to gag.

I stifled a laugh.

"Please, find a spot on the love seats," the Love Doctor said. "I will ask you four questions. You will write your answers on the flash card and pass them to me. Then, using my psychic gift, I will read your answers and determine the love match of each couple."

"Highest love match wins," Jordyn whispered.

I grinned. My cheeks hurt from smiling, as they often did when Jordyn was around.

She was so, so competitive.

Lauren and I sat on one couch, Pete and Jordyn on the other. We all grabbed a flashcard and a marker.

The Love Doctor stood in the center of the tent. She shook her hips slightly as she spoke. "Tonight, the world tilts on its side and we all tumble down, down, down. Where do you land?"

We stared at her.

Finally, Pete broke the silence. "Like in which country?"

"Or whatever, my love," the Love Doctor purred. "There are no right or wrong answers. Follow your heart."

How the heck was I supposed to answer that?

## 20

# JORDYN

*T*he first question was, if the world tilted on its side, where would you land.

I scribbled my answer:

I refuse to answer this question on account of it being stupid.

Satisfied, I handed my flashcard to the Love Doctor. She read it and the corner of her mouth twitched.

Pete looked at me imploringly. Probably trying to figure out what I wrote so he could just write the same thing and we'd be considered a perfect match. I pretended I didn't see him.

When all the cards came in, the self-proclaimed Love Doctor announced her next question. "Dream a dream of your future. Tell me lovelies, what is it you see?"

I wrote my next answer:

I see another stupid question.

Again, I was the first to hand in my answer. And again, Pete tried to sneak a peek at it. The Love Doctor plucked it expertly away, and this time rolled her eyes as she read my answer.

The third question?

"An animal spirit resides within us all. Tell me, what is the name of the animal that resides within you?"

That was easy.

Samuel Danielson.

The Love Doctor took my card and smiled the most unfriendly smile I'd ever seen. I smiled back. I was under her skin. Exactly where I liked to be. I should've been trying to do things to help me and Pete win the competition, but there was no way I was standing for this ridiculousness.

"And the final question, my loves. When the clock strikes midnight, and there's nowhere to run, to whom do you turn?"

I rolled my eyes. The Love Doctor's big quiz was basically three meaningless questions, then a fourth that asked you straight up who you loved. It was a lot of pomp and circumstance for literally nothing. She was probably just going to read the name on the card and say they're our love match.

Fine.

Two could play at that game.

I'd just write the name of my Love Match:

Samuel Danielson.

This time, the Love Doctor didn't even read my card. She just shoved it in a stack with the others. When everyone finished writing, she shifted through them, then moved around the room, her pink dress flowing behind her.

"It's been a long time since I've had four young ones that were so unique. And yet, matches you both are." She closed her eyes slowly, smiled, and opened them. "But there is one match that is much stronger than the others."

Others?

Plural?

I glanced around nervously. No one else caught what she said.

"True love is not always where we want it to be, my loves. And through my experiments, it is clear that it is, in one place, stronger than the others." She extended one hand to me, and the other to Dylan.

I did not like where this was going.

We each took her hand.

And she put our hands together.

## 21

# DYLAN

"It's just a stupid game," I shouted, tailing Lauren as she sprinted through the carnival towards the parking lot. "It's all made up. It means nothing."

Lauren spun, a storm in her eyes. "Means nothing? You've been all over Jordyn all night. I'm like your date, remember? You're supposed to be all over me. But no. You can't stop thinking about this stupid competition."

I grimaced. As much as I didn't want to admit it, I knew she had a point. While I surely wasn't 'all over' Jordyn, I probably spent too much time trying to beat her and not enough time paying attention to Lauren. But I wasn't flirting. I just wanted to prove a point. I just wanted to win.

"I'll make it up to you," I said, as we slipped through the exit, neither of us bothering to get our hand stamped for re-entry.

"And how are you going to do that? More stupid kids games? Another stupid carnival date?" Lauren nearly knocked over a pair of seniors as she stomped through the gravel lot. "You always take me on these stupid things that are supposed to be fun. It's like you think, like, we're kids.

74

But we're not kids, Dylan. We're grownups. We should dress nice and go to fancy restaurants. Not… whatever tonight was supposed to be."

"I thought it'd be fun."

"And you were wrong," Lauren said. "No one had fun tonight. You know why? Because, like, we're not twelve, okay?" She threw her hands in the air and scoffed. "Whatever. I'm done."

Done?

"What do you mean?" I asked.

"Like, it's over. I will not date someone who's obsessed with someone else."

Now it was my turn to scoff. "I'm not obsessed with Jordyn. She's just a friend. And she's Chase's sister. She's completely off-limits. Nothing can or ever would happen there."

Lauren crossed her arms. "So. Would you say she's like a sister to you?"

I paused. It should have been an easy thing to say. We grew up together. She was supposed to be like a sister to me. So why couldn't I spit out the words? Was there something else going on? No. No, there couldn't be. She was Chase's sister. I opened my mouth to speak, but I was too late.

"Thought so," Lauren said. "We're done, and I'm leaving."

I stood there, dumbfounded. This was supposed to be a cute double date, yet it ended with a break-up. It didn't hurt as much as I expected. Maybe I was just in shock. I turned to go back into the carnival, only to find Pete also on his way out.

He looked upset.

"Pete, you all good?"

"She dumped me," he said.

"What? Why?"

"Don't worry about it." Pete marched into the parking lot,

his head down, his hands shoved in his pockets. He wasn't looking where he was going and walked right into Lauren, nearly knocking her to the ground. They had a brief conversation, then disappeared into the darkness together, headed toward Pete's car.

That made sense — I was Lauren's ride. Jordyn, being Jordyn, drove herself.

I went to the entrance of the carnival, but it was being locked off.

"Can I get in?" I asked.

"Sorry, champ," the security guard said, pulling down the metal gate. "No new entries after eleven."

"Oh."

I exhaled.

And, as if the night couldn't get weirder, my phone vibrated.

A blast from Click. As much as I didn't want to deal with whatever it was, I had to look. It was a picture of me throwing the stuffed animal to Jordyn.

*Looks like someone might have taken an interest in Chase's sister. Don't boys have a code for this sort of thing?*

A second later, my phone vibrated again. This time it was a text.

Chase: Dude?

Dylan: Sorry man. It's Click. We were on a double date, Lauren didn't want the bulldog, so I gave it to J.

Chase: All good. Just thought I'd check that you're keeping an eye out for her.

## 22

## DYLAN

*I* threw eight patties on the griddle. They sizzled and spat grease onto my apron and forearms. I winced at the pricks of pain and poked the burgers with a spatula. It was a balmy Saturday evening and Beachbreak was packed. The crowd was crushing. Worse, both Luis and the other chef who was supposed to be on shift were sick, leaving me in charge of all the food preparation.

Order slips whirred by. Double cheeseburger, garden-style. Two quarter pounders with fried jalapenos and banana peppers. Veggie burger, garden-style. Six chocolate shakes, one with a scoop of peanut butter. I was scrambling as hard as I could to avoid drowning under the orders.

But, despite how insanely busy it was, everything was humming along smoothly — thanks to Jordyn. I wasn't sure if it was her competitive drive or something else, but she might have been the only person on the planet who could match Sofia's work ethic. Whenever I stepped out of the kitchen to check in on her, she was doing brilliantly.

Jordyn took orders and cracked jokes with customers. It

felt like every time I looked over, someone was laughing with delight. As soon as I rang the bell to signal that food was up, Jordyn whisked it away to the right table. Heck, sometimes she grabbed the order before I could ring the bell. Her casual demeanor was perfect for handling the very few complaints we had, and during the rare times there weren't customers, she took over the milkshake station.

In short: she was an all-star.

Time flew, and a few hours later, Jordyn turned off the 'Open' sign, dimmed the lights inside, and locked the door. She collapsed in an empty booth and exhaled. Sofia took the spot opposite her and they chatted. While they talked, I stayed in the kitchen, whipping up a quick surprise of my own.

I called it the Midnight Meal. It was the perfect thing to eat after a long shift. A burger for each of us with extra everything and two slices of melted pepper jack cheese. Fries seasoned with a sweet-hot combination of spices. And soda with a splash of vanilla. We couldn't do milkshakes because the girls had already cleaned the machine.

"Order up," I shouted, carrying the tray to the booth.

"Praise everything!" Jordyn said. She took a giant bite of her burger and sighed happily. "So good. Why don't we have these on the menu?"

"Still fine-tuning things. But if that movie comes to film in Evermore, I'm hoping I have it right by then. Maybe I can present it to their team to help us win the catering contract." I took a seat next to Sofia. "Try the fries. Different blend of spices."

Sofia shoved three in her mouth. She shrugged nonchalantly. "I could get on board with this."

"High praise, coming from you."

"It is, isn't it?" Sofia grinned. Her phone buzzed. "Luis is waiting for me. Catch you later."

I walked her to the door, ruffled her hair — mostly to annoy her — and locked up behind her. Suddenly, I was keenly aware that it was just me and Jordyn alone in a dimly lit diner.

## 23

# JORDYN

*T*he fries, the burger, the soda — it was all delicious. Honestly, I was so hungry by the end of my shift that Dylan could serve a strip of boiled leather and I would devour it.

Burgers and fries? Even better.

Dylan sat across from me and picked at his fries. His Beachbreak apron was still tied around his neck. It made him look cozy in the cutest way possible. Like a guy who'd bake you cookies, then curl up next to the fireplace with you.

*Whoa. Jordyn. Red light. Where did that come from?*

I choked on my fries, then tried to disguise my choking with a cough.

"Easy, Jones. Not sure my CPR is up-to-date."

I sipped my soda, then finished coughing. "Because that's what I want — to be lying on my back while your mouth — with you — I mean — while you're trying to — the point is, let me die."

Dylan laughed. "You'd rather die than get CPR?"

"Depends who's giving the CPR."

He chuckled and stretched. Rather than untying his

apron, he lifted it over his head. The bottom of his apron tugged at his shirt, revealing just the tiniest hint of tanned, smooth abs.

Very, very nice abs.

*RED LIGHT, JORDYN. RED FREAKIN' LIGHT.*

Dylan glanced at me, a confused expression on his face.

Oh man, had he caught me checking him out?

Not that that's what I was doing.

I would never, I repeat, NEVER, check out Ramirez. He was my brother's best friend. I'd known him basically my entire life. And that was all he would ever, ever be. Even if he had muscles and abs.

*JORDYN, SERIOUSLY. RED. LIGHT.*

Dylan mowed down his fries. "Can I ask you a question?"

"Didn't really give me an option, did you?"

"Always so clever," he said, smiling.

I inclined my head slightly. "Well, since you were so polite… go ahead."

His eyes met mine. "At the carnival — why'd you break up with Pete?"

"Who says he didn't dump me?"

"He wouldn't dump you. That would've meant he had to tear down his shrine. And he worked so hard on it."

I laughed, then took a sip of my drink. I had a choice to make. I could lie, crack a joke, and we could move on with our lives. Or I could tell him the truth. I decided on the latter — Dylan deserved the truth. "Promise you won't do anything stupid."

"We both know I can't promise that." Dylan rapped his knuckles against his head. "I've taken a few too many hits to not do anything stupid."

"Fine. If you do something stupid, I'll blame it on a concussion," I said. Okay. Here goes. "After the Love Match game, when you and Lauren got in that fight, Pete... he tried to film it."

Dylan looked puzzled. "Film it? Why?"

"He wanted to put it on Click. With a hashtag that him and I were the best couple."

"Seriously?"

"Seriously."

Dylan took a bite of his burger, considering the information. He dabbed at his mouth with a napkin. "And you dumped him."

I nodded. "He should know how I feel about Click. It blasted Chase. It blasted Hailey. No chance I will let it put someone else in the crosshairs. Especially not a friend. And..."

Dylan waited patiently. It was such a pleasant change. He wasn't trying to anticipate my next sentence. Wasn't waiting to throw his jacket in a rain puddle for me to step over it. In short, he wasn't trying to save me, to keep me in a glass case like some valuable autographed football. He was just listening and letting me be me.

"And he didn't get me," I said. "He had this vision of me. Of who he wanted me to be. And he was nice, so it's not like he was forcing me to be that person or anything... but it's like he ignored everything about me that wasn't part of his vision. He liked the idea of me, but not actually me. And when someone only likes the idea of you, sooner or later, they will find out the idea of you isn't the real you, and then they'll break up with you anyway. So really, I did us both a favor."

Dylan finished his burger and leaned back. "Profound, Jones."

"Only because I'm tired." I drank the last of my soda. "And what about you? What went down in the parking lot?"

"Lauren?" Dylan shrugged. "It was never gonna work.

Same thing, really. She wanted us to be this super classy, super adult couple. She wanted our dates to be at museums and art galleries. I'm a bit too hard-headed for that."

"Yeah," I agreed, "I really don't think you'd understand art."

"I could understand art."

"Could you, though?"

"If I wanted to."

I smirked. "Sure. You could TOTALLY understand the complexities of art."

"Like you understand it."

"I'll have you know I went to a paint night once."

Dylan looked at me innocently. "And I suppose because you can complete a connect-the-dots that means you can sketch, too?"

"Pfft — have you seen me with the mazes on the kids' menu? I SLAY those."

"They're designed to be easy so kids feel a sense of accomplishment."

"Good," I said. "I feel very accomplished."

Dylan laughed.

We sat in a companionable silence, the kind of quiet you can only enjoy with someone you'd known for most of your life. My mind wandered. I didn't have a shift tomorrow, but the forecast called for rain — and lots of it. I didn't feel like stumbling through the mall for twelve hours, so I would likely be trapped with my parents for most of the day. I hoped they wouldn't argue too much. Or at least not too loud. That way—

"You okay?" Dylan asked.

"Sorry. Just thinking."

"About?"

I sighed. "Trying to find a way out of the house tomorrow. You sure I can't cover a shift? You don't even have to pay me."

"Don't think that's legal," Dylan said. "But if you really want to get out of the house — I can hook you up."

"How's that?"

"With an old Ramirez tradition." He winked. "If you're willing to take a chance."

## 24

## JORDYN

*R*ain pattered against my bedroom window. Outside, the sky was a dismal grey, the streets slowly filling with puddles. There was no thunder, no lightning. Just rain.

Aside from the steady rainfall, and sometimes a slight burst of wind through the trees, there was no noise, either. Both of my parents were home, but they were keeping to different areas of the house. It still felt like things could explode at any moment, but at least for now, things were quiet.

I hopped off my bed and paced through the dirty laundry that covered my floor. Beneath my hoodie and shorts, I was wearing a bathing suit, as per Dylan's instructions. Despite my incessant protests, he wouldn't tell me what he had planned. And believe me — I begged.

Jordyn: Tell me.

Jordyn: Please.

Jordyn. What about now?

Jordyn: I'll bake you cookies.

Jordyn: Better yet — I'll let you bake ME cookies.

Jordyn: Tell me.

Jordyn: Are we there yet?

Jordyn: Come on.

Jordyn: Please? I'd tell you. Maybe.

Jordyn: Dylllllaaaaannnnnn. It's Jordddyyyynnnnn. Tellllll meeeee.

Dylan: Do you want me to block your number?

Jordyn: Only after you tell me.

But, despite my best efforts, Dylan kept his mouth shut. So I was reduced to waiting.

Every time a car drove by our house, I scurried to the window to see if it was Dylan's. Nervous energy bubbled inside me. I was excited to get out of the house. Excited to see Dylan. And not the normal excitement that comes with seeing a friend. This was something else.

Something more.

My phone vibrated.

Dylan: Here.

Jordyn: I'm not coming outside unless you TELL ME.

Dylan: Leaving in five.

Ugh.

Fine.

## DYLAN

*I* drummed my fingers on the steering wheel as I waited for Jordyn to emerge. When I pulled up to her house, I had a moment of doubt. Was I supposed to knock on her front door? Honk my horn? Send a text?

When did a simple hang out session with Jordyn start to feel so complicated? And more importantly, WHY was it starting to feel so complicated? If Chase was there, I would've sent them both a text. I wouldn't have even thought about it. So why did things feel different?

The front door opened and Jordyn popped out.

Sauntering through the rain, she adjusted her ponytail. Unlike other girls, she didn't bring an umbrella or pull her hoodie over her head. In fact, she didn't shield her hair from the rain at all. She just let it fall, smirking all the way.

And her cute, defiant smirk was making my heart do some very uncomfortable things.

Jordyn hopped in the car. "So. Where are you whisking me off to?"

"I've come this far, you think I'm going to give it away?"

"Yes."

"You know me better than that, Jones."

Jordyn buckled her seat belt. "And you know how persistent I can be."

I cranked up the radio until it was so loud she had to cover her ears. I yelled above the music. "What's that? I can't hear you."

Jordyn reached for the volume.

I swatted her hand away. "Driver picks the music!"

I shifted into gear, and we pulled away from her house.

# JORDYN

*M*ercifully, Dylan let me turn down the radio as long as I promised not to badger him about where we were going or what we were doing. I didn't love surprises, but I hoped that Dylan knew me well enough not to surprise me with something I didn't want. We talked as we drove. Our conversation had an almost strange, practiced casualness to it. It's like we were both avoiding anything too deep.

We followed a winding road through the foothills as Evermore fell behind us. The windshield wipers slipped across the glass as the rain thundered down. After forty-five minutes of driving, we passed an old wooden sign. It read:

Lake Evermore

I looked at Dylan like he was a crazy person. Because he was. "A lake day? In a rainstorm? Is there something you're not telling me, Ramirez?"

"There's a lot of things I don't tell you, Jones," he said. "For starters — did you know every member of the Ramirez family was born with gills?"

I snorted. "You know that makes you a mermaid, right?"

"Technically, the term is 'merman'," Dylan said. "And what we're doing today is a Ramirez family tradition. I told Sofia the plan and she almost — ALMOST — wouldn't let me bring you. Took a lot of convincing. And half my tips. We don't get to do it that often, either. This is the type of thing you can only do while it's raining."

My curiosity was piqued. What on earth could you only do at a lake while it was raining?

We pulled into an empty parking lot, the tires rumbling over gravel.

"Leave your clothes in the car so they don't get wet. You'll want 'em for the drive home." Dylan hopped out of the car and whipped off his t-shirt, revealing a well-defined set of muscles underneath. I felt an instinctive urge to give his abs a quick jab to see if they were as hard as they looked, but instead I quickly looked away — after taking one last peek — and climbed out of the vehicle.

I stripped down to my bathing suit, feeling self-conscious as I did. My body suddenly looked even more skinny and flat chested than usual. Lauren, for all her shortcomings, at least had cleavage. I knew that everyone was self-conscious about themselves now and again, but this was the first time in my life that I could remember feeling self-conscious about being in a bathing suit near Ramirez. We had spent every summer in my memory together, running around spray parks and jumping in outdoor pools. So why did I suddenly care what he thought about what I looked like?

You know why, Jordyn.

Shut up, brain.

Dylan opened the trunk. He heaved a giant roll of plastic sheeting out, like the kind professional painters used to wall off areas. It must have been at least six feet wide.

"Confession: I don't love that you brought me to the middle of nowhere, and the first thing you do is pull out a giant roll of plastic. Is there a shovel back there, too?" I looked past him, but there was no shovel in the trunk. Only a few small canvas bags, the kind you use for tent pegs, and a hammer.

"What do you—"

"Patience, Jones," Dylan said. "Good things come to those who wait."

"Good things come to those that take them."

Dylan grinned. He nodded towards the tent pegs. "Grab those and close up."

I did.

Carrying the giant roll of plastic sheeting over his shoulder, Dylan led me to the top of a small — but steep — hill that overlooked the lake. He set down the roll of plastic, found its edge, then extended his hand.

"Pegs and hammer."

I handed them over.

The plastic sheet, I saw now, had been modified to have several metal ring holes along its edge. Dylan inserted the pegs through the holes and hammered them, pinning the sheet to the ground. When he was finished, he unrolled the plastic another ten feet down the hill, then repeated the process, putting in more pegs.

When I realized what he was doing, I was more excited than a puppy going to its forever home.

"WAIT. NO. SHUT UP. IS THIS—"

Dylan laughed. Unwrapped another ten feet of plastic sheeting. Pinned it to the ground. "Now you're getting it, Jones."

"SHUT. UP."

Dylan was making a gigantic Slip 'n Slide.

# DYLAN

*W*e stood at the top of the hill and admired our work. The plastic sheeting — modified by myself, Luis, and my dad — stretched from the top of the hill, across the beach, and into the lake. It was close to a hundred and fifty feet long, with pegs holding it down at ten-foot intervals. I couldn't count the amount of times my family had come out to this hill on a rainy summer day and set up the Ramirez Slip 'n Slide.

It had taken three summers to perfect. If the plastic was too thin, it tore. If you used the wrong camping pegs, you'd pull them out of the ground — or worse, they'd snag you on the way down. Even the angle you put them into the ground was important. I'd learned that lesson the hard way, and I still had a scar on my calf to prove it.

Jordyn stared at the sheet in awe. "Ramirez, this might be the most impressive thing I've ever seen."

"Not bad, right?" I smiled with pride. "Dad and Luis made the first one when I was seven. We were supposed to come out here for a regular lake day, but it was pouring rain. Mom insisted that we go anyway. Luis and I were whining that the lake had nothing fun to do in the rain. We wanted to go somewhere with a water slide."

I grinned. I remembered Luis and I complaining the entire drive to the lake, dad getting more and more angry. "When we finally got here, dad was so mad. He had this giant plastic tarp leftover from doing renovations at Beachbreak. He threw it on the ground and shouted: you want a water slide, you make one! Then he stormed off. So, Luis and I fiddled with the plastic sheet. We put some sand piles on it to hold it in place. When Dad came back, he almost died laughing. He said he was joking, that we weren't actually supposed to make one. But… the tradition stuck."

Jordyn smiled. It wasn't her usual smile, the one that was part smile, part challenge. It was softer, warmer. "I wish my family did things like that," she said. "The only time we're together is when we're at one of Chase's football games. Or when we're at a restaurant trying to pretend we're a happy family."

Without thinking, I put my arm around her shoulder and gave her a half-hug. We both looked out over the lake, the water rippling under the rain.

"So," I said. "There's a rule you need to know about. So you don't get hurt."

"And what would that be?"

"Easy," I said. "Last one in the lake loses."

# JORDYN

*S*illy, silly, Ramirez. You have to get up pretty early to pull one over on Miss Jordyn Jones. I expected Dylan to pull some kind of stunt, to try to make a getaway. So when he did, I was ready.

I wrapped my arms around his waist and clung to him the way a barnacle clings to a ship. Together, we stumbled and slipped over the wet grass, half-wrestling, until we reached the edge of the Ramirez Slip 'n Slide.

As soon as our feet touched plastic, we both lost our balance. I flew through the air, looking like a cartoon character that slipped on a banana peel, and landed hard on my butt. Ramirez landed beside me.

Then gravity took over.

We started sliding towards the lake.

No, not sliding—

Careening.

Completely out of control.

But even the threat of tearing up the Slip 'n Slide couldn't stop us from fighting. We both wanted to be the first one in the water. Badly.

I grabbed Dylan's shoulder and pulled as hard as I could, trying to sling shot myself past him.

Sliding on his back like a turtle, Dylan reached out and clutched my ankle.

Tried to pull me back.

I laughed, planted my foot on his forehead, and tried to push off.

The world blurred as we sped down the hill.

We hit the beach.

We were almost at the finish line—

Dylan, now with a wet heel print on his face, made a desperate grab for my other ankle. He pulled as hard as he could, practically climbing me like I was a tree. He wrapped his arms around me.

I squealed with delight and struggled to break free, feeling the warmth of his body against mine.

But he was too strong.

His foot caught the plastic, and we spun so that he would hit the water first.

He laughed triumphantly. "I—"

KERSPLASH.

We hit the water together, our momentum completely sapped, and we tumbled awkwardly, flipping end over end in the coldness of the mountain lake. Even underwater, our hands found each other, wrestling against one another.

We broke the surface together, Dylan's arms around my waist, my arms around his neck. Somehow, my legs were around him too.

We were both laughing like maniacs, and I had the almost insatiable urge to rest my head on his shoulder, to—

*DANGER, JORDYN. DANGER.*

In the laughter, our eyes met. I'd never been this close to Dylan before. Never looked this deeply into his eyes. They were warm and inviting, like a spot by the fireplace after a freezing November day. There was a kindness to them I'd never noticed.

And a spark.

All the feelings of my childhood crush rose to the surface, a volcano about to explode. The crush that had never truly gone away, but had been buried deep, dormant, was once again alive, the dangerous heat of the lava dancing all over my skin.

Dylan's dark eyes were locked on mine, a whirlpool of emotion.

Were we going to—

*DANGER, JORDYN!*

Without thinking, I lurched backward, kicked off Dylan's chest, and swam to the beach, safely locking my feelings back down where they belonged. I needed to keep those buried.

"You win round one, Ramirez," I said, crawling out of the water. "Best two out of three?"

We spent the rest of the day together. We trudged to the top of the hill, then raced and wrestled our way to the bottom. At some point, we stopped keeping score — probably for the first time in my life. When we tired of racing, we started taking on ridiculous challenges.

I tried to surf the entire way down.

Dylan rolled down the hill like an egg.

I sat cross-legged and pretended to primp my hair and take selfies.

Dylan went on his knees and flexed his biceps, posing like a fitness model.

Throughout the day, rain poured.

And I never wanted it to stop.

## 29

# DYLAN

*I* pulled into the Beachbreak parking lot. Luis was already parked. There was a car beside his, one I had not expected to see—

Dad's.

"This can't be good." I shifted into park, turned off my car, and headed for the back entrance. Even before stepping inside, I could hear Luis and Dad arguing over something. They weren't shouting, but it was heated.

A tingle of dread crawled across my back. The only person more stubborn than my brother was my dad. Their arguments lasted so long that pages blew off the calendar and seasons changed. Mom liked to joke that they started arguing when Luis learned to talk, and they hadn't stopped arguing since. I took a deep breath, shouldered open the door, and let their voices wash over me.

"You need to rest," Luis said firmly. "Get strong."

"I am strong," Dad replied, a hint of anger in his voice.

"You know what I mean."

"The doctor said to rest for two weeks. It has been over two weeks. I am ready to make my return."

"You were supposed to be off all summer."

I carefully closed the door behind me. They were arguing in the kitchen, no doubt while prepping food for today's shift. I imagined them carrying out their debate, sharp knives and heavy meat tenderizers in their hands. The last thing I wanted to do was go into the kitchen and step between them, but I knew I didn't have a choice. Some things needed to be dealt with.

I tied my apron around my neck and entered the kitchen.

Dad immediately turned to me, an enormous smile on his face. "On time, as always. Now, tell your brother I'm ready to work."

I hesitated. Any hope I had at avoiding their argument had been dashed almost immediately.

Dad looked at me expectantly. "Well?"

I sighed. I knew exactly where this conversation was going. It was a train set on its tracks, barreling towards disaster. How long would Dad freeze Luis out this time?

"You were supposed to take all summer off."

Dad's eyes narrowed, and he frowned. "You too, then?"

"We want you to get better," I said. "You need to rest. If you come back too soon—"

Dad waved away my protests. "Rest, rest, rest. That's all anyone wants. Beachbreak was not built on rest. It was built brick by brick with blood, sweat, and a side of mortar. If you want anything in life, you must seize it. I taught you both this."

Luis and I exchanged an uneasy glance. What were you supposed to say to the owner of the restaurant? How could we stop Dad from doing what he wanted to do — even if it meant he risked his own health? Mom could reign him in, but calling her would escalate the argument to nuclear proportions. Best to handle this ourselves.

If we could.

"We just want what's best for you," Luis said. He kept his voice soft, like a man approaching a growling dog. "That's all."

"Don't you think I know what's best for me?" Dad snapped. "A Ramirez does not quit. They work until the work is done. And when there's an opportunity on the horizon, they bear down until they are ready. Beachbreak must be ready. We must be ready."

"Opportunity?" Luis asked.

"The movie," Dad said, his voice growing louder. "Some action star is coming to Evermore. Acting and directing some big movie. They want local catering. It'll be a big contract — biggest in Beachbreak's history. We get this contract, we can make summer profits in the slow season. We do that, it's the start of a franchise."

So that was why Dad returned. If the rumors were true, and the movie really was coming to Evermore, the contract would have a massive financial reward. Not to mention any bonus publicity that came with being a caterer for a major motion picture. Dad probably saw this as his best shot to get the financial push he needed to set up a second franchise. That had been his goal for as long as I could remember.

It was a goal he'd sacrifice everything, even his health, for.

We couldn't let him do it.

"We have it under control," I said.

Dad shook his head slowly. "You've made me proud. But something this big? I need to be here for this. I need to come up with something—"

The office door swung open.

Jordyn waltzed in wearing her Beachbreak uniform. Her hair was pulled through the back of a black Beachbreak baseball cap. How long had she been listening?

"Family gathering?" She smiled and extended her hand to my dad. "Jordyn Jones."

Dad shook her hand. "The new waitress. Chase's sister?"

The corner of her mouth twitched.

I wanted to bury my head in my palms. The Joneses had been visiting Beachbreak for years. Heck, Jordyn had been at our house countless times. But Dad couldn't remember her? No wonder she got so angry. I would've been angry too if people I knew my entire life referred to me as 'Luis's brother.'

"That's me," Jordyn said. She kept her voice pleasant, which was impressive, given how she must be feeling inside. "I take it you're here to try Dylan's new recipe? The one for the movie?"

No, Jordyn, no! What was she doing?

Dad raised his eyebrows. "A recipe for the movie?"

"It's not ready," I blurted.

Jordyn eyed me skeptically. "Tasted ready to me. And it's incredible. It's called the Midnight Meal. It's what you eat after a long shift at work — or a long shift on set. It'll be perfect."

"You're inventing new recipes?" Dad asked. His voice was the calm of embers ready to flare into fire. He didn't like it when we branched out.

Jordyn either didn't bother reading the room or didn't care, because she continued on, undeterred. "It's so, so good. You will try it, right?"

Dad nodded slowly. "I just might."

Uh oh.

♥

THIS WAS BAD.

Nervous energy flooded through me as I worked in the kitchen. I fried a burger, melting two slices of pepper jack cheese on top. I prepped the toppings, then made my blend of sweet hot spice and powdered the fries. After putting everything together, I carried it to my dad's booth.

He rubbed his chin. "Does it taste as good as it looks?"

"Better," Jordyn said. She sat in the booth across from him. While I was preparing the Midnight Meal, she was chatting him up. I was too focused to hear much of what she said, but I heard them both laugh. That was a good sign. Jordyn looked at me, pouting playfully. "You didn't make me one?"

"I didn't think—"

"Never mind that," Dad said. He popped a pair of fries into his mouth. Chewed, turning them over with his tongue. He washed it down with a drink. His expression was stoic, giving away nothing. "Intriguing blend. Cayenne?"

"And a light touch of brown sugar and chili powder," I said. "I'm still trying to find the balance between sweet and hot."

Dad ate another fry. "You can taste too much brown sugar. Cut it down, bump up the chili powder. You want a hint of sweetness, but you don't want to know what it's coming from precisely. It needs to blend with the fire."

I made a mental note and tried not to let the disappointment show on my face. I knew it wasn't perfect, I just wanted Dad to—

"But it's good," Dad said.

Good? That was obscenely high praise coming from Dad. I smiled.

He took a bite of the burger. Closed his eyes. Swallowed. "And this... this is very good."

I beamed, miraculously resisting the urge to pump my fist and dance around the room. Very good? I don't think he had ever called something very good before.

"You call this..."

"The Midnight Meal."

"The Midnight Meal. Adjust the spicing on the fries. But

this… this is exceptional. A Ramirez works for their opportunities. You do well with this, and you can present it to the movie people." Dad wiped his hands off on a napkin. He carried the tray to the counter and packed his food in a to-go box. "Your mother will want to try this."

"I can make—"

"We can share," Dad said. "If this is the work you're doing when I'm not around, it is very impressive. Both of you. As such, I guess my back can rest a little longer."

"We won't let you down," I said.

He smiled. "You never do."

## 30

# DYLAN

*I* sat in the back office at the end of a long shift. The place was packed, again. And once again, Jordyn and Sofia carried us over the finish line. They'd even started a friendly competition against each other to see who could get their customers laughing the most. Beachbreak had never felt so welcoming.

I double-checked a ledger that listed the ingredients we used and completed the order for next week.

Jordyn came into the office. We hadn't talked all day.

"Busy shift," I said.

"'Tis the season. Sofia said you wanted to see me before I punched out? You're not sick of me, are you?" She was joking, but there was an ever so slight hint of fear in her voice.

"Not yet." I took a drink of water. How was I supposed to thank the person who did the impossible? I didn't know, but I had to try. "Dad's a good man. But he's difficult. He's never — NEVER — taken a step back from Beachbreak. Then, in you come, getting through to him. I wanted to thank you.

From me and Luis. We've agreed to give you our tips for the night."

With a flick of her wrist, Jordyn shooed the idea away. "So dramatic, Ramirez. You keep the tips. Your burger got the job done, not anything I did."

"He wouldn't have tried it if you didn't suggest it."

Jordyn shrugged. "Literally the least I can do."

I didn't know what to say.

Jordyn raised an eyebrow. "You okay?"

"You want the honest answer?"

"Always."

I drew a deep breath. "What if I present the Midnight Meal to the movie people and they hate it? What if they don't give us the contract? What if everyone believes in me, and I fail?"

Jordyn pursed her lips. She sat in the chair opposite me, reached across the desk, and squeezed my hand. "Then you fail. Happens to the best of us. Or at least, that's what they tell me."

I laughed. "You don't fail?"

"I'm basically Superman."

"I knew it."

"Of course you did." She gently squeezed my hand. "You made a good burger, Ramirez. As stupid cheesy as this sounds, I believe in you. And if you don't believe in yourself, that's fine. I'll just believe in you enough for both of us. Sound good?"

Warmth fell over me. "Thank you."

"No problem." Jordyn let go of my hand… and flicked me in the forehead.

"What was—"

"Sorry," she said. "We were getting too personal. We have to maintain a professional distance. You know how it is." She winked, stood, and just like that, left me smiling like an idiot.

There was nothing better than having someone like Jordyn Jones in your life.

## 31

## JORDYN

*I* left the restaurant with one thought echoing through my mind:

What kind of idiot flicks the boy they might have feelings for in the forehead?

CRANK THE VOLUME LOUD ENOUGH, and rock music drowns out everything. Greta Van Fleet, Green Day, Foo Fighters. Find the right song, turn the volume as loud as it goes, and fade away into bliss while lying on your bed.

At least, that was the idea.

Unfortunately, even a killer guitar riff or an amazing drum solo couldn't drown out the shouts of my parents. They were yelling at each other again. Someone slammed a door, and the house shook.

I turned up the volume. My phone warned me that cranking the volume any louder risked doing permanent damage to my ears. Good. I'd take permanent damage to my ears if it meant I didn't have to hear my parents yelling at each other. I closed my eyes and let Dave Grohl's voice carry me away—

The house shook again. A classic mom move — slamming the door twice to make a point.

There were some problems rock music couldn't solve.

I needed to get out of the house.

When my parents fought like this, there was only one place I could go: the Jones Family Drive-In. I tore the white sheet from my bed, folded it, and stuffed it in my knapsack. Headphones still blaring, I slipped down the hall to Chase's room. In his closet, he had a ball of yellow rope, a Ziplock bag of clothespins, his laptop, and the projector. Everything I needed for a private movie night.

I took off the headphones. My parents didn't care where I went, not really, but they wouldn't let me leave the house this late at night. They had to at least give off the illusion that they cared.

I creeped to the top of the stairs and listened carefully. They were in the kitchen arguing over… it didn't matter. I figured I was less likely to need therapy when I was older if I didn't listen too closely. Quiet as a shadow, I slipped down the stairs and grabbed Dad's keys from the bowl by the front door.

A thick manila envelope sat beside the bowl. The return address mentioned Schwartz & Sterling. Sounded like a legal firm.

*Red light, Jordyn.*

I stood still, a deer frozen in the headlights. My fingers hovered over the edge of the envelope. It would be so easy to lift the top, to pull the document out and confirm my suspicions.

I shook free of my trance.

No.

Not tonight.

Not when I was by myself.

♥

MY PARENTS either didn't notice or didn't care when I started Dad's car and pulled out of the driveway. My car was wedged in front of his, so I did what any sane person would do and jacked his. I ripped through the neighborhood, found the exit to the highway, then cranked my Spotify playlist as loud as it would go. The bass made the car shake, and I suspected the speakers would blow at any minute.

I hoped they did.

What was in that envelope?

Schwartz & Sterling.

I mean, what else could it be?

Schwartz & Sterling.

It had to be—

JORDYN. RED. LIGHT.

Ugh. I couldn't think about that stupid manila envelope. Not right now. I settled into cruise control and drove down the highway. On the entire drive, I didn't see a single car. Tonight, I truly was all alone.

After a half-hour of driving, I took the car off cruise control, took a quick exit, and pulled into an empty field. I drove over a rough patch of grass to a spot where two trees stood, about fifteen feet apart. I strung the rope between the two trees, then attached the sheet using clothespins. I put my spare blanket on the hood of the car. The metal was still warm from driving.

I plugged the projector into the laptop and angled the image onto the sheet. I didn't have popcorn, but that was okay. I didn't need popcorn. Or Chase.

I was Jordyn Jones. I didn't need anyone or anything.

I put on an episode of Friends. It was the show I watched when I didn't know what else to watch. It was the easy escape.

But this time, the escape didn't come.

I'd never been at the Jones Family Drive-In alone. Only with Chase. And now, with no one by my side, parked in the middle of nowhere with nothing but the moon and stars for company, I felt completely alone. And cold.

"Pull it together," I said, hugging my knees to my chest. "You're fine, Jordyn. You're fine."

I breathed through my teeth, fighting back the tears that were threatening to come. "Don't be a baby," I said. "You're fine. You knew this would happen. You. Are. Fine."

My voice was pathetically weak.

I picked up my phone.

I expected to call Chase, but my fingers had a mind of their own, and they scrolled right past his number, landing on a different one. I dialed.

Ring.

Ring.

Ring.

Click. A voice on the other end. "J? What time is it?"

"Midnight," I said. I opened my mouth to say something else, but something was stuck in my throat, so instead, I stayed quiet.

"You okay?" Dylan asked.

Control yourself, Jordyn. You don't want him to think you're a crazy person.

I breathed slowly. "I didn't know who to call."

"What is it?"

Oh, it's so many things. "I'm going to send you my location."

"J?"

I ended the call.

The phone was a blur, but through my traitorous tears, I found Dylan's contact and sent him a pin with my location.

## 32

## JORDYN

*I* was halfway through my third episode of Friends when I heard the low hum of an engine pulling off the highway. A few seconds later, a car's suspension creaked as it bounced over divots in the field. A car door opened, closed.

"Jones?" Dylan walked softly towards me.

"Present." I sat on the hood of my dad's car. I shifted to the side, leaving room for Dylan, and patted the blanket, inviting him to sit.

"I'm wearing jeans," Dylan said. "Might scratch it."

"It's my dad's."

"Okay." Dylan climbed on the hood of the car. He said nothing. Instead, he subtly reached for my hand, interlocking his fingers with mine. His hands were rough, but they were warm. Comforting. The feel of his hands in mine was almost enough to break through the dam of emotions I'd been holding back.

"I..."

I, what? How was I even supposed to begin? I couldn't, so instead, I swallowed my words.

"It's okay," Dylan said. "You don't have to talk if you don't want to."

I nodded, still not able to speak. I shifted closer to him, the blanket bunching up between us, and rested my head on his shoulder. He smelled like fresh rain.

Dylan let go of my hand and looped his arm around my shoulder, pulling me close to him.

It felt right, and being this close to him gave me the courage to voice the unspeakable.

"I think my parents are going to do it this time," I said. "Like they're actually getting a divorce."

Dylan squeezed me closer, gently resting his head on mine.

"I don't know what to do," I said.

"You don't have to know what to do."

"Chase would know what to do."

"Chase would call me," Dylan said.

That was true. When Chase needed something and I wasn't around, he always turned to Dylan, didn't he? Or Abby. But I didn't have an Abby to fall back on. I did have a Dylan. "Oh. Then maybe I did know what to do."

"What are friends for, if not midnight movies?"

My throat was dry, my voice barely above a whisper. "Thank you. For coming."

"Always."

I cuddled into Dylan, and we watched the rest of the episode in silence. When it was done, my tears were dry, and for the first time since I saw the envelope, I wasn't thinking about my family's impending destruction.

I was thinking about Dylan.

He came for me when I needed him the most. He understood me more than anyone I'd ever met. More than Chase, even. He understood that he couldn't fix what was happening. He knew that I couldn't fix what was happening even if I wanted to. And he didn't try to fix everything. He didn't tell me everything was going to be okay because he knew that it wasn't. He just sat with me in silence and let me be broken.

And that was amazing.

I tilted my head and looked up to him. We weren't far apart.

"Do you think... do you think love ruins friendships?" I asked. "Like my parents? Does it always end up that way?"

His eyes met mine. His hand was still on my shoulder. "Depends on the friends."

I inched closer. His scent, the smell of fresh rain, was almost overpowering now. I wanted to lose myself in it. "Hypothetically?"

For the briefest of moments, his eyes flickered to my lips. "What do you think?"

What did I think?

I saw what happened — what was happening — to my parents. It was clear:

Love ruined friendships.

But here, sitting on the hood of a car with Dylan, anything — even love — ruining what we had seemed so impossible. So distant. My heart beat so fast I was sure that he could hear it. Some distant voice was telling me to stop, was telling me to pay attention to the red light.

"Love ruins everything," I said. There was no conviction in my voice. "That's why some things can't happen. Even if I wanted them to."

"Right. Some things can't happen."

And yet, we couldn't stop staring at each other.

Dylan reached up, brushed a strand of hair from my face. His hand didn't leave my cheek. "And there's rules," he said.

"There's rules."

"Like your best friend's sister... she's off-limits."

"Rules like that," I agreed.

My heart beat faster.

"Hypothetically."

"Hypothetically."

We inched closer together, almost intoxicated. It was getting harder and harder to breathe.

"That's why some things can't happen," I repeated.

Dylan rubbed his thumb on my cheek. "Because…"

"Because…"

Dylan pulled me close.

His lips touched mine, and I was swept into a summer rainstorm. I felt the breathtaking chill of water trickling down my back, the coolness of rain washing over me. Goosebumps rose on my arms.

He pulled away.

His eyes found mine. They were full of questions. "Is this… okay? Are you okay?"

I was more than okay.

"No one finds out about this," I whispered. My heart was pounding out of my chest.

"No one," he agreed, his voice rough.

And that was all I needed to hear.

I put my hand on the back of his neck and pulled him towards me. Our lips met, perfectly fitting together. I leaned back, feeling the coolness of the windshield on my lower back, contrasting with the warmth of Dylan's body on mine.

Something so wrong had never felt so right.

## 33

# DYLAN

*I*t was only ten in the morning, and I was on my thirteenth cup of coffee. The coffee was so strong that if you put a spoon in it, the spoon would stay standing. Honestly, I needed the caffeine. I hadn't slept much. Every time I closed my eyes, I thought about Jordyn.

I had kissed her. And I'd liked it.

More than liked it.

What did it mean? What was it supposed to mean? Were we still friends, or were we more? My thoughts rampaged, the noise drowning out everything around me.

I had no idea what it meant, but I knew one thing for certain: I wanted to do it again.

I tried to check the inventory, but I found myself repeatedly opening the same boxes and marking off the same columns on the tablet.

Dude. Get it together.

Jordyn would arrive soon. And when she did, I planned to ask her out on a date. A real one. It felt like there was something between us, something real, and I figured the only way to know if she felt the same was to take my shot.

Thinking about asking her made me nervous.

The coffee didn't help.

I poured my last cup down the drain, found a package of mints, and stuffed one in my mouth, crunching furiously. Couldn't ask a girl out with coffee breath, could I?

I was just starting to calm my nerves when the back door opened.

Jordyn waltzed in. Threw her jacket on the coat rack. It fell to the floor. She glared at it, picked it up, and tried again. It stayed up this time. "Ramirez."

"Jordones."

Jordyn smirked and raised her eyebrows. "I'm sorry, what was that?"

"Shut up."

"You're so charming in the morning."

"I haven't had my coffee," I lied.

Way to go, Dylan. Way to start everything off as awkwardly as possible. And how was she acting so calm, so normal?

I cleared my throat and closed the door. The office suddenly felt smaller than usual, like there wasn't enough space in here.

"Oh, a closed door," Jordyn said. "Am I in trouble? Or are you hoping for a repeat of the other night?"

How could she be so casual? It was almost infuriating.

"It's not like that," I said. I took a step towards her. "Well, it is. But not like, right now. I want…"

"Spit it out, Ramirez."

I let out a groan of frustration, and before I even knew what I was doing, I closed the remaining space between us, my lips meeting hers.

The world spun as I kissed her. Kissing Jordyn was, well — wow. Kissing other girls hadn't felt like this.

When I finally broke the kiss, I looked down at her. What was she thinking?

Her blue eyes met my stare defiantly.

It was now or never.

"I want to take you out on a date. A real date."

## 34

## JORDYN

*a* date with Dylan Ramirez?
A real date?

I eyed him to figure out if he was teasing me. He wasn't. Of course he wasn't. We'd shared something special the other night. He'd just kissed me again, a kiss that felt passionate, sincere. Teasing me when I was at my most vulnerable would've been terrible, and it's not something Dylan would do. He could practically read my mind. Did that bother me? I wasn't sure.

But if Dylan wanted me to go on a real date with him... he was serious. He thought there was something between us.

Was I ready for something like this? This was the only boy I had ever felt real feelings for. The only boy who had ever made my stomach fill with butterflies, made my heart skip a beat. If I was being honest with myself, deep down, I had wanted this for a very long time. And now that it was happening, I was scared.

Fear was not an emotion I liked to entertain.

I took a deep breath and kept my voice low, trying way

too hard to sound casual. "If we're going to go on a date — a real date — I have some conditions."

"Like?"

"We have to keep it a secret," I said simply. "From my brother. From your family. From Click. From everyone. Right now, everything feels like magic. But when people find out, when all of this becomes real, everything breaks. And I don't want this to break. Not yet."

It was probably the most honest I'd ever been. I felt intensely vulnerable.

Dylan smiled. "So, let's do it. Let's keep it a secret. From Click. From everyone."

I wanted to kiss him again. Instead, I did my usual Jordyn maneuver and pretended to examine my nails. With boys, you couldn't appear too excited. It scared them away. "I'd like to see how you're going to keep our date a secret, Ramirez. Especially when I have some anonymous jerk trying to blast me across Click."

"I've got a few tricks up my sleeve," Dylan said. "Meet me here tomorrow. Midnight."

"Tomorrow at midnight," I agreed.

❤

MIDNIGHT. What kind of time was that for a first date?

Answer: the perfect time for two people doing everything they could to keep that date a secret.

What, exactly, did a person wear for a midnight date? In fact, what did a person wear for any date?

I thought about video calling Hailey, queen of the outfits. But if I did that, I would have to tell her I was going on a date with Dylan freaking Ramirez. I wasn't sure if she'd scream or laugh or simply refuse to believe me. And I wasn't sure I was ready for any of those reactions.

I could hardly believe it myself as I stood in the center of my room in a bra and jeans, hopelessly flipping through my closet for the right shirt. My nerves jangled. This was all so new, so exciting, so forbidden — and the way Dylan kissed me made me feel a way nobody ever made me feel before.

So here I was, sneaking out of my house at midnight tonight.

A jolt of anticipation buzzed through me as I remembered the electric feeling of Dylan's lips on mine, the way his hands had tangled in my hair as he pulled me close to him.

All I knew is I wanted him to do it again.

And again.

And again.

I tried on three tops before settling for a floaty blue tank with ribbon spaghetti straps that emphasized my dark blue eyes. I fishtail braided my hair the way Hailey had taught me and only stabbed myself in the eye twice with my mascara wand. Satisfied, I slicked on some coconut lip gloss and called it good.

Or at least, it was as good as it would get.

I slipped on my Vans and crept past my parents' room and downstairs. All the lights were off, but one glance at the driveway confirmed my dad wasn't home. Where was he? With who?

I pushed all thoughts of my parents away as I started my car and backed out of the driveway with my headlights still off. Tonight wasn't about them, it was about Dylan and me.

The thought made my heart pound.

The drive to Beachbreak couldn't have taken more than fifteen minutes, but it felt like it took fifteen hours. Every light was red, and somehow, despite it being near midnight, there was traffic throughout Evermore.

Finally, I arrived.

Dylan was waiting outside the back door, casually leaning against the wall. He was wearing a black sweater that showed off his athletic, muscular frame and complemented his olive complexion. He smiled slowly as he took in my appearance, his eyes crinkling at the corners. Butterflies swarmed my stomach. I could hardly believe how much the world had flipped on its head in the past few days. Dylan Ramirez, hot football running back, serial cheerleader dater, and my childhood crush and bath time buddy, was smiling like that for me.

His eyes met mine, and he smiled again. "You look beautiful."

I did? The words sounded so strange, coming from the mouth of the boy I'd known all my life. I waited for him to follow his compliment with a jab. When he didn't, I looked to the sky and pretended I wasn't blushing furiously. "You're not so bad yourself."

"Follow me."

We walked around Beachbreak to the secret set of stairs that lead to our outdoor, riverside patio. It was nearly impossible to get tables there. Unfortunately, it was also exactly where someone trying to capture me for Click would look. If he was planning for us to eat on the beach, it wasn't going to work.

Ugh.

I couldn't believe how much I wanted this to work. How much I wanted Dylan to not disappoint me. A midnight dinner on the beach was romantic, but—

There were no tables set up on the beach. No picnic blanket. Nothing at all to show what he had planned.

Maybe we were just going for a walk?

"Give me a sec," Dylan said. He practically dove through a patch of nearby bushes, reaching for something. He found what he was looking for, grunted, pulled, and emerged from the bushes dragging a large raft. He hauled it to the water's edge, careful to ensure that it didn't float away.

The raft looked familiar.

"Where did you get that?" I asked.

"Hailey kept it around after Trey had his Riverwalk concert," Dylan said. He dove back into the bush, and this time pulled out a bottle of sparkling apple juice, two plastic wine glasses, and an insulated bag. He took my hand and helped me on the raft. It wobbled slightly, and I fell into his chest.

He grinned. "As if that wasn't intentional."

"You wish, Ramirez," I snapped before quickly turning away. Since when did being around Dylan make me blush so much? Was this annoying trend the start of something larger?

I took the bag of food. "Thanks. You can go now."

"Funny," he said, a hint of laughter in his voice. He went back to the bushes one last time and emerged with a paddle. He hopped on the raft and pushed us away from shore.

The river pulled us into the current.

Once we were away from the shore, it was surprisingly cold, and I shivered.

"Check the bag," Dylan said.

I did. Inside the bag, next to something that smelled delicious, was a black, oversized Panthers hoodie. The name 'Ramirez' was etched into the shoulder, along with Dylan's number 30. Without asking permission, I put the hoodie on and savored the warmth. It smelled like him.

"You've thought of everything, haven't you?" I asked. "Did you write a song to serenade me with? That's what Trey—"

Before I could finish my sentence, Dylan started singing. Loudly.

And obnoxiously.

"Someone will hear," I whisper-shouted.

That only made him sing louder.

I glared, tackled him, and put my hand over his mouth.

"Can't stop this singing voice, Jones," he said through my fingers, before starting to sing YET AGAIN.

There was only one way to get his painfully obnoxious singing to stop. I took my hand away from his mouth, leaned in, and kissed him.

The singing stopped.

But as soon as I pulled away, he took a deep breath, ready to belt out another show tune, which, of course, forced me to kiss him again.

"We can keep going like this all night," Dylan smirked, then threatened to break into song again.

"I can't do this all night," I whispered. "The food smells too good."

"Always thinking with your stomach, Jones."

"Obviously. Why else would I spend so much time with you?"

Dylan laughed. He pulled the food out of the bag and set it on the raft. For the evening, we'd be dining on two Midnight Meals with chocolate shakes as a side. And for dessert? New York-style cheesecake, purchased from a mom and pop bakery on Main Street.

It was exceptional. Each bite was a complete explosion of absolute deliciousness. The adjustments Dylan made to the recipe? Perfect. If I could have married that meal, I would have.

We floated along the river, the Riverwalk and Beachbreak disappearing behind us, replaced by thick forest. There were a few hiking paths along the edge of the river, but no one would be on them this late at night. Dylan had figured out the perfect date, an ideal combination of the two things I craved: food and privacy.

Dylan handed me a tiny fork for the cheesecake. "How are you doing with everything with your parents?"

"Trying not to think about it."

"Sorry."

I took a bite of the cheesecake — delicious, obviously — and waved away his apology. "It's fine. I mean you asking is fine. Honestly, I'm trying to be all casual about it, but it's hard. Really hard. Harder than I ever thought it would be. And I know how stupid it sounds because Chase and I have been saying that we want them to get divorced. But now that it's actually here, actually happening, I just..."

In the ultimate gentleman's move, Dylan set his unfinished cheesecake aside so he could put his arm around me and hold me against his chest. "It's okay for things to be hard. And you don't have to pretend things aren't hard. Not around me."

I rested my head on his shoulder, continuing to eat my cheesecake. "I know."

We finished our food, continuing to drift deeper into the forest. The conversation drifted with us. He told me more embarrassing stories about Luis, and I wasn't ashamed to cackle like a hyena. I didn't have any embarrassing stories about Chase to share — Dylan knew all of those already. I briefly considered telling him one about Hailey, but I didn't want to sacrifice her pride.

The river pulled us into the lagoon.

An incredible sight greeted us.

Hundreds — maybe thousands — of fireflies danced in the sky. Their reflections shimmered off the slow water.

And off Dylan's eyes.

I traced my fingers along his temple, then wrapped my arms around him, pulling him into me. We settled into a comfortable balance of kissing and chatting while the fireflies flew around us. It almost didn't feel real.

"Do you ever wonder what will happen when everyone gets back?" I asked.

"All the time," Dylan whispered. I felt his voice on my lips. "But maybe we don't have to worry about that right now. Maybe right now, all we have to worry about is each other."

"Maybe you're right." I pulled back briefly, looking him in the eye. "You have to promise that whatever happens, we'll still be friends. No matter what."

"I promise."

I kissed him. "This, whatever this is, I don't know yet, but it's just for us."

"It's just for us," he agreed.

As long as it was just for us, as long as the outside world didn't intrude, everything could stay perfect for a little while.

## 35

# DYLAN

*P*ressure meant different things to different people. Sometimes, it made people crumble. Sometimes, it made them into diamonds. I'd always loved everything that came with pressure. When we were marching to the end zone, and there was only time on the clock for one more play, I wanted Chase to put the ball in my gut and let me lower my shoulders and plow through defenders on my way to the game-winning touchdown.

Working at Beachbreak was a different pressure. There were no screaming fans. No band that struck up the school fight song whenever we served a burger. It was more of a constant, unceasing pressure. And not everyone could take it.

I stood in the kitchen and examined a menu for what must have been the millionth time. During the height of summer, Luis and Dad liked to change the menu around. This year, they wanted to add my Midnight Meal to the mix. It would be the first time a meal I created would end up on the menu. It needed to be perfect.

I carefully measured out a few more spices for the fries, adjusting the ratio of chili powder and brown sugar just as

Dad had recommended. I quickly stirred them together, then spooned the spices over a fresh batch of fries. They were still hot, so the spice stuck to them easily.

"Lemme." Jordyn burst between me and the fries, grabbed two, and popped them into her mouth before I could warn her. She chewed with her mouth open, fanning the invisible flames now dancing on her tongue. "Hot! Hot!"

I laughed. "That's what you get for trying something before the cook tells you you're allowed."

"Worth it," she mumbled. She snatched a cup, filled it with Sprite, and downed it. Steam hissed when the cool liquid hit her tongue. "That's better," she said.

"So? What do you think?"

Jordyn checked to make sure no one was watching, then swung her arms around my neck and gave me a quick kiss.

I smirked. "That good, huh?"

Before she could fire back a sarcastic retort, I pulled her towards me again, pressing my lips against hers and kissing her one more time.

When we finally broke apart, my hands lingered on her hips as I caught my breath.

"You have a gift," Jordyn said, smiling up at me.

I smirked again.

She hit me. "I didn't mean that. Arrogant much?"

I laughed. "Whatever you say, Jones."

I reluctantly slipped out of her grasp. Luis was outside taking a break and would come back in any minute, and while Sofia was busy with a customer, you never knew when she would sneak into the kitchen for something. Jordyn and I were determined to keep our relationship — or whatever this was — a secret. The less people knew about it, the less it could go wrong.

So far, we'd been lucky. Quiet kisses in the kitchen, subtle squeezes in the back office, lingering hugs — no one had caught on. And no one had captured our relationship for Click. Whoever was trying to uncover Jordyn's secrets had either decided to lay low, or they'd gotten bored. Either reason worked for me. As long as our relationship remained in a cloud of secrecy, we would be okay. But as soon as that cloud blew away—

No need to think about that. Just live in the moment.

A boy's voice carried through to the kitchen. "I'm with Under Cove Films."

My heart shot into my chest. Under Cove Films? That was the name of Christopher Lyons' production company, the one that was planning to shoot in the Denver area. They were already here?

As casually as I could, I sauntered over to the milkshake machine, pretending to examine it so I could eavesdrop. A boy, roughly the same age as Sofia, stood at the counter. They were chatting. She was leaning forward so hard I thought she would fall over the counter, and the smile on her face was way too big to be fake.

"And you're with catering?" Sofia said. She was trying to play things cool, as if she didn't care about movies at all. Almost as if she had never even seen a movie before. But her body language gave her away. She was fidgeting nervously under the counter as she talked, her hands shaking slightly.

"Sort of," the boy said. He had a lilting British accent. "I'm with the movie. My dad has a meeting today, so he sent me to check out Main Street for lunch. They're renting an office a few blocks away. I'm supposed to bring back some food."

Sofia raised her eyebrows. "Is your dad... sorry, never mind. What can I get you?"

Is the boy's dad who?

I briefly glanced over my shoulder to get a better look at the boy. He was tall, blond-haired and blue eyed, and definitely bore more than a passing resemblance to Christopher Lyons himself.

No.

It couldn't be, could it?

Christopher Lyons' son? Here, at Beachbreak?

"Dylan?"

"What?"

Sofia held out an order.

"Right." I snatched the order out of her hand, taking it back to the kitchen. Luis was back from his break. I handed him the order slip. "This one's important — it's going to the cast and crew for that new movie that might shoot in Evermore. If we do well here— "

"You don't have to tell me," Luis said.

We immediately got to work. Burgers and topping sizzled as Luis worked the grill. I made a fresh batch of fries and mixed a fresh blend of different spices. Jordyn was at the milkshake machine. She was going above and beyond, too. She topped each milkshake with a perfect dollop of whipped cream, found a jar of maraschino cherries, and put one on top. They looked incredible — straight out of the '50s.

But, while we were all working to make the best meal possible, Sofia was smiling and laughing with the boy on the other side of the counter. She was quick-witted, and if the amount of times she laughed was any sign, so was he.

"Hmm," I said, eyeing the pair. I didn't like the way she was talking to him. Every protective urge I'd ever had was rising through my body, telling me to put a stop to whatever was going on between them. But I couldn't. Intellectually, I knew that neither of them was doing anything wrong. They were just kids.

Kids that were flirting.

And flirting lead to dates.

And dates lead to kissing.

And I was definitely not ready to see my little sister go on a date. She was only 15! I mean, sure, I had gone on dates when I was 15. But it was different.

I caught Jordyn's eye as she delivered the shakes on a cardboard tray. She was watching me, barely containing her laughter. She told the oh-so-witty boy that she'd check on the food and be right back.

"What?" I practically growled at her when she came into the kitchen.

She grinned maniacally. "You. Look. So. Mad. You better not let him see you like this. Honestly, Ramirez. You look like he's a linebacker and you want to crush him."

"So what?"

"I think someone's feeling a bit overprotective."

"I am not," I lied. I tried to look past Jordyn to see what was going on between Sofia and her new best friend. Conveniently, oh so conveniently, Jordyn positioned her body to block my view. I couldn't say for sure, but I thought I saw the boy hand Sofia his cell phone.

Wait.

WAS SHE GIVING HIM HER NUMBER?

"Is the food done?" I snapped at Luis.

He gave me a weird look. "You hungry or something? You're acting a little hangry."

"We need the service to be quick so we can impress this..."

Jordyn and Luis both stared at me and waited for me to finish my sentence. Jordyn, in particular, looked deeply, deeply amused. Luis didn't see what the big deal was. But he couldn't see what was going on at the counter.

"This what?" Jordyn asked innocently.

I gritted my teeth. "This very important client."

"Uh huh. Sure."

"Maybe you could take over," I suggested. "Send Sofia back here."

Jordyn was practically shaking with silent laughter. "Oh, I don't think that's necessary. I think she's definitely got it all under control."

"It's not funny."

"You're right. It's hilarious." Her eyes glittered. "She's only a year younger than you. You dated girls when you were her age. So let her flirt with the cute boy."

"He's not cute."

"Oh, okay," Jordyn said. "I suppose Dylan Ramirez is the expert on what makes a cute guy."

"He's awkward looking."

"Yes," Jordyn agreed. "It's super awkward to be six feet tall, have the jawline of a movie star, eyes bright as diamonds, and abs that I suspect are chiseled out of marble. How terribly awkward. You should probably save your sister before she's forced to spend any more time with that awkward statue of a man."

A brief bit of jealousy flared in my stomach. Jordyn found this random guy cute, too?

"Looks like someone got under your skin," she said, her voice sing-songy.

"It's not that. It's just that no one is supposed to date my sister." Still feeling a smidge overprotective, I boxed up the awkward boy's food and brought it out of the kitchen. I placed it on the counter.

"Thanks," the boy said. His smile was friendly.

Mine was forced. "No problem. New to the area?"

"Sort of."

"Cool," I said. I grabbed a menu and stashed it in the bag. "In case you want to order something later. We're open all day."

"Thanks," the boy said. He turned to Sofia. "And thank you. You've been wonderful."

Sofia went pink as an embarrassed cartoon character.

"Bye."

I watched the boy leave.

Ugh.

Being a brother could be so complicated.

## 36

## JORDYN

*J* stormed across my bedroom, magically resisting the urge to throw everything I owned on the floor. Anger simmered through my body as I replayed Dylan's comment: "No one is supposed to date my sister."

Why?

Because they're not allowed. Because he was her big brother and he was supposed to protect her.

I understood the protectiveness. Really. I did. It was nice that he cared about Sofia. But to say that no one was allowed to date his little sister, and to cast her as completely off-limits? What did that say about what Dylan thought about me? He was Chase's best friend. Was that all I was to him? Some piece of forbidden fruit? Was I, yet again, going to get reduced to being nothing more than the sister of Chase Jones?

ARGH. I wanted to hit something. Hard. Over and over I had begged my parents for a punching bag. Pillows had way too much give — I wanted something that you could feel when you punched it.

This is a healthy way to express yourself, Jordyn. Violence. Just like mom.

The thought leaped into my head, unprompted and unwanted. And it just made me angrier. So what if I was a little like mom? Did that really matter right now?

Before I could get even angrier, my phone vibrated on my desk. I picked it up, saw there was a notification from Click, and briefly contemplated throwing it through the window. Heck, I was so angry I could probably throw it through the wall. I imagined a row of little cell phone shaped holes going through the walls all the way into the yard. The thought made me smile, and fortunately, it also calmed me down.

At least slightly.

I unlocked my phone and opened Click, bracing myself for the worst.

As usual, Click did not disappoint.

The blast showed who else: Dylan and me. He had his arm over my shoulder, a big smile on his face. I was frowning and holding my stuffed animal, Samuel Danielson, protectively. This photo was followed by another, one of us standing outside Beachbreak before one of our shifts. Dylan was leaning into me — not quite touching, and I was on my tiptoes, looking directly into his eyes. The final shot? Us inside Beachbreak, laughing, my hand resting on his arm.

This last image was followed with a caption:

*When the cat's away, the mice will play. Wonder what Chase Jones thinks about his twin sister being spotted just about everywhere with his best friend?*

I swore. Bit my lip.

I'll admit — it didn't look good. Three pictures with me and Dylan, spread across the summer, all showing us close together. But none of them showed us kissing. Sure, we were touching, but no more than close friends would touch. If anyone — i.e. Chase — asked about our relationship, we could lie. Tell him that Click was just trying to stir up drama. After the app had tried to sabotage him last fall when he was dating Abby, he'd have to believe us.

Right?

My phone vibrated again. This time it was a text message from Dylan.

Dylan: You see Click?

I debated not texting him back. After his 'no one dates my sister' comment, I wanted to give him the cold shoulder and really let him stew. But, if we got the blast, Chase would get it too. And when he started asking questions, Ramirez and I needed to have our stories straight. My brother might be a jock, but he wasn't stupid. And he wouldn't let me get away with playing dumb.

Despite that, I was definitely not in a hurry to jump at Ramirez's beck and call. If he wanted to talk, he had to work for it.

Jordyn: You come here. I'm free.

Dylan: On my way.

Good.

Maybe we'd have time to have ourselves a little chat about the merits of dating someone's sister.

## 37

## DYLAN

The heat of the July sun did nothing to dispel the frigid breeze that surrounded me as soon as I arrived at Jordyn's. While she could always be moody and had a habit of glaring, the way she was today made it feel like there was a thick wall of ice between us. I didn't know why it had formed, but I would do my best to pick my way through it. The first step? A warm and welcoming hug.

I opened my arms, ready to pull her into me—

But she spun on her heel, rebuffing me completely. "There's no one in the backyard."

I followed her through the house. Both of her parents must have been at work. That was good — I wasn't a very good liar, and knowing them, they were no doubt trying to keep their divorce a secret. Even Jordyn wasn't supposed to know.

We sat on the patio beneath an oversized striped umbrella. Jordyn pulled a free chair across the deck, the metal legs scraping against the wood. She put her feet up. She wore a pair of large sunglasses which made it difficult for me to see her eyes. It was like she was wearing a mask.

What was wrong?

What had I done?

I cleared my throat, feeling very uncomfortable. "So. Click."

"Click," she said. "We need to get ahead of this. Figure out what our story is and get it straight. Chase hasn't called yet, but he's going to soon."

"I don't want to lie to him," I said.

"Like you could even if you wanted to," Jordyn replied. Her expression was still flat, still unreadable. "But, let's say you were going to tell the truth. What would you say?"

Talk about putting me on the spot. My cheeks burned. Jordyn knew how I felt, didn't she? The last thing I wanted to do was sit in the backyard and have the least romantic confession of feelings of all-time. "You know how I feel."

"I do?"

"Don't you?"

Her mouth twitched. "I'm Chase's sister. Which means you're not supposed to date me. Because no one is supposed to date someone's sister. Disregarding how that would make all of human society completely collapse."

What?

Where was this—

Oh.

OH.

That explained the wall of ice between us. When she heard me complaining about the awkward boy's interest in Sofia, she must have assumed—

"It's not like that," I said.

"But it is," she snapped. "At least a little."

"I don't like you because you're Chase's sister. I like you because... because you're Jordyn."

Her expression softened almost imperceptibly. She sighed. "Maybe — maybe — I'm being too hard on you."

"Thank you."

"But that doesn't change the facts."

My stomach sank. She was right. No matter how I felt, it didn't change the fact that she was still, ultimately, Chase's sister. And Chase probably wouldn't be super thrilled that, as soon as he left town, we became more than friends. Much more. "What do you want to do?" I asked.

"I don't know," she said. "I know I don't want this to end."

"So we keep going," I said. There was a subtle edge of desperation in my voice. I knew our relationship — whatever it was — was living on borrowed time. But borrowed time was still time. We could still be together. "We keep going, at least until Chase gets back. And then... I don't know what we do then. But we don't need to figure it all out right now."

Jordyn bit her lip. She looked like she was puzzling over what I had said, weighing all the options. Finally, she nodded. "We keep going. Leave it all to the future, I guess. But I still have a problem. Someone is trying to put me on Click. We need to figure out who."

"The last blast showed us in three places," I said. "We need to figure out who would have been at all three places — and who would have wanted to put you on blast."

"That's the problem," Jordyn said. "Anyone could've taken the photos of us at Beachbreak. Especially given that you're Mr. Popularity. And the carnival? Same thing. Could've been anyone."

"Great," I murmured. "So we've narrowed down our suspect list to literally anyone in Evermore. Can you think of anyone who would have a reason to throw you to the wolves? Maybe Pete?"

"QB2? I doubt he'd have it in him to do anything malicious. He practically worshiped me in the most annoying way possible. Revenge isn't his style." Jordyn took off her sunglasses. Polished them on her t-shirt. "What about Lauren?"

Lauren? That was a possibility. We hadn't exactly ended our relationship in a good place — and she definitely blamed Jordyn for that. "It's not impossible," I said. "What about Madison? One of the other cheerleaders?"

Jordyn shook her head. "I'm her ex-boyfriend's sister — far too low on the totem pole for Madison to bother with. Same with the other cheerleaders. And they probably wouldn't take a shot at me because they'd be afraid of making Chase angry."

We sat in silence for a minute, each of us scrolling through our phones, trying to put together potential suspects.

"So, Lauren's the only realistic option," I said.

"She was at the carnival," Jordyn said. "She's come into Beachbreak. And she hates me. Why not her?"

Before we could dive deeper into the conversation, the patio door slid open. It was Jordyn's mom. Her salt and pepper hair was pulled back into a bun, and she wore a perfectly pressed, white linen sundress and matching cardigan. Her red-lipsticked mouth parted in a smile as she saw me. She was the epitome of polished. And though she and Jordyn shared the same navy eyes and angular, beautiful faces, Mrs. Jones was a precisely crafted oil painting while Jordyn was a rainbow of modern art splatters.

"Dylan! Wonderful to see you here," Mrs. Jones said. A panicked expression crossed her face. "Jordyn's not in trouble, is she?"

Jordyn sighed heavily. "You know it's possible for people to want to visit me because they like me, right? Not just because I'm in trouble?"

"Of course, dear," Jordyn's mom said. The panic didn't

leave her face, and she kept her eyes on me, waiting for me to confirm the worst in her daughter.

"We're just visiting," I said, mustering my friendliest smile.

"That's good. It's nice that Chase has someone who can check in on our Jordyn. Someone that he can trust. I'll get some freshly squeezed lemonade." She left, sliding the door closed behind her.

Her words echoed in my mind. Chase has someone he can trust...

But if he could trust me, then why was I working so hard to lie to him?

## DYLAN

*J* stood in the kitchen at Beachbreak, my stomach twisting into a thousand nervous knots. My hands sweat, my fingers leaving prints on the order slip. It was supposed to be so easy. A Midnight Meal, a double-cheeseburger, garden style, and three buckets of fries, each with a different spice. Jordyn had already made the shakes.

I double-checked all the ingredients, then carefully placed the burgers in their paper bags, trying to angle them in the most appetizing way possible. I grabbed the tray and carried it out to the three people sitting with Luis in the back booth. Luis was wearing his regular Beachbreak uniform. But the other three men were all in clean, pressed suits. Suits that looked way too hot — and way too expensive — to be in Beachbreak.

I set the food on the table. "Here you go."

The men nodded their thanks and immediately appraised the food. The nearest, a tall, skinny man with a face so tan it was practically leather, took a bite of one burger. Chewed. Swallowed. "More than satisfactory."

I breathed a sigh of relief. This entire time, I'd been terrified that they would hate the food. That my failure as a chef would single-handedly cost Beachbreak its opportunity to cater the movie.

A woman — I think she was a location scout — popped a handful of fries in her mouth and chewed them greedily. "More than satisfactory, Mike? These are great!" To emphasize her point, she devoured another handful. "We'd be happy to have Beachbreak be the official caterer for Under Cove Productions' next film."

I nearly leaped with joy.

"But."

But? There was always a but, wasn't there?

"We're not making that decision today," the man — Mike — said. "We have a few more restaurants to trial. At least one of which is another burger place."

"Okay," Luis said. He folded his hands in front of him, looking like a kid pretending to be a businessman. Originally, Dad planned to be here to meet the movie people. Then they showed up a day early for lunch without telling us who they were until they'd already ordered their meal. "Is there anything else you need from me?"

"The menu," Mike said, offering a thin-lipped smile. "We need to know that you can cater to all dietary restrictions. While we wouldn't be using Beachbreak every day, we like to have a selection of local options available for lunch, and we would likely use your restaurant as our official caterer at least once a week, if not twice."

Seemingly out of nowhere, Jordyn arrived with a menu in hand. She passed it to Mike, then gave me a wink as she walked away.

"Can I get you anything else?" I asked.

"Could use more of these fries," the woman said.

Mike rolled his eyes and waved me away, his Rolex glinting as it caught the sunlight. "That'll be all."

I returned to the back. As I was walking past the office, I heard voices. Jordyn and Sofia.

"I was hoping Noah would be here today," Sofia said.

Noah. So the awkward British boy and Sofia were on a first name basis, were they?

"Better luck next time," Jordyn said.

I peeked through a crack in the door. Sofia was sitting on the edge of the desk, eating her lunch. She had a distinct look of disappointment on her face. She probably expected that awkward boy to come back with the movie people. That would explain why she'd been hogging the mirror all morning. But how would she have known?

Unless they were texting.

I didn't like the idea. But I thought about what Jordyn said. Sofia should be able to date if she wanted to. And if I continued to act all over-protective, all I would do was push her away. I decided against bursting into the office and demanding she stay away from all boys until the end of time.

"Do you want some advice?" Jordyn asked.

"Sure."

"Make your move soon."

Sofia hesitated. "Why?"

"Because the longer you wait to make your move, the more complicated it gets," Jordyn said. "You get a crush on someone, and you bury it because you know you're not supposed to have it, or because you're afraid he doesn't like you or whatever. And then you become friends. And in my experience, the closer you are as friends, the less likely the relationship is to work. I've honestly never seen close friends date and have the relationship end well."

I slipped away from the door before they realized I was

listening. Now my stomach was twisting into knots for a whole new reason. Was that what Jordyn thought? Was that how she felt?

Did she think this relationship — whatever it was — was ultimately doomed?

## 39

## JORDYN

*I* flicked off Beachbreak's neon 'Open' sign, turned the deadbolt, and rested my forehead against the warm glass door. It was another long shift and my feet were aching, my head pounding. In the summer, it didn't matter if it was a weekend or a weeknight, Beachbreak was busy. The customers were friendly but loud, and just before closing, an entire youth soccer team had stopped in, their coach carrying a giant trophy.

In the back, Dylan was cleaning the kitchen. He seemed off tonight, a strange and uncomfortable distance growing between us. Something was bothering him. Every time I tried to ask him if he was okay, he blew me off. Which contributed to my admittedly foul mood.

But now, there was nowhere for him to escape.

When I saw Dylan scrubbing down the grill, every frustration evaporated. He was so tired, he looked like a zombie. His eyes were half-closed, his head barely propped up. He hunched over the grill and rubbed his back, looking for the briefest of moments like his father. The last thing he needed right now was to deal with me attacking him.

I slid up beside him and bumped my hip into his. "Dead man walking."

He grunted in response, not taking his eyes from the grill.

I checked to make sure no one was watching. "Need a kiss to bring you back to life, Sleeping Beauty?"

The words felt awkward as soon as they left my mouth. I was trying to be cute and flirty, but I felt more like a kid playing pretend. And doing a poor job of it.

"Just a nap," Dylan said, in no mood to engage in any banter. Or kissing.

Was he pulling away from me?

I didn't know what to say, so instead of breaking the silence, I let awkwardness fill the space between us. It was tremendously uncomfortable. Worse, I couldn't tell if he was being honest that he was just tired or if he was mad at me. Or both. Maybe he needed some space. Maybe having me around all the time was too much Jordyn for him to deal with. I could be a handful. I think the only person who could have me around constantly was Chase.

"I think I know how we can find out who's following you," Dylan said. He still didn't look up to meet my eyes.

My ears perked up. "How?"

"We'll go on a fake date." Dylan finished scrubbing the grill and went to the sink to wash his hands. "Lure them out into the open."

"You want to go on a fake date to hide our real relationship?" I asked. Oh, the irony. I thought going on a fake date was a silly idea. But going on a fake date pretending to be in a relationship to hide your real relationship? Trying to understand it immediately made my headache worse.

"Yes." Dylan said simply.

"And where would we go on this fake date?"

"Somewhere cheesy. Romano's?"

"And if we don't see whoever's following me?"

"Sofia," Dylan called.

His sister stumbled into the kitchen. Normally she was a ball of energy, but the long shift and the endless number of customers had even worn her out. "What's up?"

"We need your help." Dylan explained the plan. He would take me on a fake date to Romano's, reserve a table on the Riverwalk patio. Sofia would watch from afar to see if anyone was taking pictures of us. She would film everything. Then we'd review the film to see if we noticed anyone.

When he was finished explaining, Sofia gave him the type of eye-roll that only a little sister could pull off. "I'll do it, but this is stupid. Why do people care if you're dating? And are you even dating?"

"We're not," Dylan said tiredly.

"Too bad," Sofia replied. She shot me a wink. "You couldn't do any better than Jordyn."

I grinned. "You hear that, Ramirez? Your sister is a certified genius."

♥

I EXAMINED my outfit in the mirror and wondered what Dylan would think.

It was pretty, yes, but it didn't feel like me. The navy floral sundress was flouncy and girly. The shoes — beige espadrilles my mom had bought me that still had the tags on — felt pinched and uncomfortable. My hair fell in loose waves around my shoulders, but I longed to yank it back in its usual messy ponytail.

When was the last time I cared this much about what a boy would think about how I looked? It was never like this with Pete. With Pete, I did what I wanted, when I wanted, and let him suffer the consequences. I probably wasn't the best person for him to date.

And now I was going on a fake date with the guy I wanted to be my real boyfriend.

Boyfriend.

Was that what I wanted?

I ripped the price tag off my shoe with a snap. It was pointless to deny any of my feelings. They were definitely there, and they were making my life way more confusing than it should've been. I wanted to be with Dylan, but Chase would be back soon. And with Chase came reality. And we'd agreed — when he came back, our fling needed to end.

Didn't it?

I knew this in my head, but yet, in my heart—

*WHOA. Red light, Jordyn.*

The doorbell rang, the sound echoing through our empty house.

My heart fluttered. I checked my outfit one last time.

"Okay. Here I go." Trying to steady my breathing, I slowly made my way to the front door. I rested my hand on the doorknob, took one more deep breath, then pulled it open.

Dylan flashed me a bashful grin that was entirely different from his usual cocky smirk. Why did he have to look so ridiculously hot in dress clothes? He wore a white shirt, khakis, and a navy blazer. His hair was neater than usual, curling at the nape of his neck, above his collar.

His hand was behind his back.

I eyed him suspiciously. "Got something planned, Ramirez?"

"Nothing you can't handle." He presented me with a bouquet of lilies in an array of vibrant pinks and purples. They were the color of clouds during a beautiful sunset.

Oh. Oh wow. My cheeks flamed red.

I took the lilies from him, and, because I didn't know what else to do, I smelled them, then held them against my chest. I didn't know what to say. I wasn't the type of girl to have a favorite flower, or to even tell the difference between different flowers, but the gesture almost overwhelmed me. Would this have felt different if we were going on a real date?

Dylan looked at me cautiously. "They're not too girly for you, are they?"

"They're lovely," I said, my voice soft.

"Do you know how to take care of them?"

"Shove them in water?"

Dylan laughed. "Kind of. Here."

He took the flowers from my hand, the foil crinkling in his grip. We went to the kitchen and found an empty vase in one of the cupboards. Dylan unwrapped the flowers, cut the stems at an angle, then plunked them in the water.

"Does it matter if you cut them at an angle?" I asked.

"Gives them more surface area, makes it easier to drink," Dylan said. "At least that's what my mom said."

I raised an eyebrow. "Do you only know how to do this because you asked your mom?"

He grinned sheepishly. "Told her I had a big date."

"And she told you to get flowers?" I tried to hide the disappointment in my voice.

"Flowers were my idea. Thought they were pretty. According to the florist person, lilies symbolize purity, commitment, and... uh..."

"And what?"

Dylan cleared his throat. "Fertility."

I burst out laughing, resting my arm on his shoulder as I bent over, gasping for breath. Touching his shoulder felt so natural, so normal, that I didn't even think about it. My nerves for the date melted away as I choked with laughter.

"Fertility? You want me to be fertile?"

"That's not what—"

Tears in my eyes, I took the vase from him. "Can't wait to tell my dad you bought me fertility flowers."

"They're not fertility flowers! They're just pretty!"

"Uh huh, sure." Still laughing, I took the vase up to my room. I cleared a spot on my desk and set the vase there. He was right, the flowers were pretty. Beautiful, even. Pete said a lot of nice things, but this was the first time a boy had given me flowers. As much as I wanted to tease him endlessly that he'd given me 'fertility flowers,' the gesture meant a lot.

It may have been a fake date, but nobody was here to see him give me those flowers.

It was one more thing he did for me that he didn't have to do.

One more thing he did for me just to make me happy.

I sighed, smiling.

Stupid Ramirez.

## 40

# JORDYN

*I*n Evermore, Romano's was the cliché place to go for a cliché date. It was exactly as cheesy as the name implied. The tables were draped with white cloth. The napkins had pink hearts etched around the edges. On each table, there were flickering candles for ambience, but the candles used LEDs instead of open flames. If you sat inside, there was a large glass room with a grill so you could watch your steak being prepared. Italian love songs played through the speakers.

And, if you asked, they would shape your meal so it looked like a heart.

It was like love had puked all over the place.

I hooked my arm in Dylan's as the waiter — who I suspected was faking an Italian accent — led us to our table, which was on the Riverwalk patio. We were right near the edge, in plain sight for the entire world — and for whoever was trying to blast me all over Click.

It was strange to be sitting in plain sight, clearly on a date with Dylan Ramirez. I felt like I was being torn in half. Part of me wished that this could be a real date, that we didn't have to hide our relationship from anyone. And the other part of me didn't want to get my hopes up. If you kept your hopes low, it hurt a lot less when everything came crashing down around you.

And everything always came crashing down. Just look at my parents.

Dylan cleared his throat. "So… how are you?"

"Good. You?"

"Good."

"That's good."

"Yeah."

On the drive over, we listened to the radio. Probably because neither of us knew what to talk about. The invisible distance seemed to grow between us. It was so strange how you could be right beside someone but feel so far apart. Was this what love did to friendships? Made conversation super awkward?

"I, uh, I don't know what to talk about," I said. "Do you… come here often?"

Dylan examined the menu. "First time. Always walked past it, never been inside. My dad doesn't like it. Says the food is overpriced fancy bull—"

Our waiter cleared his throat, a thin-lipped smile on his face. "Have you decided?"

"Oh, yeah," Dylan said awkwardly. "I was just talking about this other restaurant."

"Certainly, sir."

We ordered our food. Dylan opted for a steak, medium-rare, side of Caesar salad. I ordered the carbonara. This wasn't a real date, so I could shove my face full of pasta, right?

While we waited for our food, neither of us tried to make conversation. Instead, we both stared at the river as it gently flowed. I had hoped I was imagining the distance between

Dylan and myself, but the more time we spent together, the more obvious it was: something was wrong. For the first time in my life, I legitimately felt awkward around Dylan. For the first time ever, we had nothing to talk about, laugh about.

And I hated it.

Was it because Chase would be back soon?

Was it because of something I did?

Was it because of something Dylan felt?

I glanced at him, trying to read his mind, but his expression was stoic. Our fake date had started so promisingly with the flowers, but now, it didn't feel romantic at all. It didn't even feel like friends having dinner.

It felt like watching my parents have dinner. Two people, pretending to love each other, just going through the motions. Trying to hold on to something that wasn't there anymore.

We finished our meal. Dylan's dad was right. The food was fancy, overpriced, and not particularly satisfying. I wished we had gone to Beachbreak instead. Or literally anywhere else.

"Would you like some dessert?" the waiter asked.

"Up to you," Dylan said.

I held my stomach. "I think I'll pass."

"Just the bill," Dylan said. After the waiter left, he looked at me, concern in his eyes. "You okay?"

"Not feeling too hot, but I'll be alright." I wasn't lying, not entirely. I didn't feel great, but it had nothing to do with my stomach. It felt like I was staring at a window and watching a crack slowly form and crawl across the glass. Soon, with the right amount of pressure, everything would break. I would break.

Dylan paid the bill, ignoring my insistent pleas to pay my share, and we strolled along the Riverwalk. Truthfully, I'd only been half paying attention to see if anyone noticed us while we were on our 'date' but I had seen no one take pictures.

Dylan sent a text.

A moment later, Sofia emerged, seemingly from nowhere.

"How are the lovebirds?" she asked.

Dylan grimaced. "See anything?"

"Oh, do I have a video for you." Sofia played the video on her phone. Sure enough, as Dylan and I sat at our table and awkwardly looked out at the water, someone strolled through the patio, pausing to snap some pictures.

Someone very, very familiar.

I saw red.

"They are DEAD." I growled.

## 41

## JORDYN

*I* stormed up the sidewalk, my fists clenched. The short drive over to the two-story house had done nothing to help me cool off. If anything, it made my anger worse. I thought of all the things I'd like to do to claim my revenge, and quite frankly, there were too many to list. I reached the front door and knocked so hard that the house shook.

"I will kill him," I said. "I'm going to freaking kill him."

"Not if I kill him first," Dylan said from behind me. The entire night had been awkward, but at least now we were united again. Anger did crazy things.

"Open up!" I banged on the door. "Open the door!"

There were footsteps inside, then, a moment later, the door swung open. Standing on the other side was the person responsible for everything. The person who'd made it their goal to put me on blast on Click all summer. The person I thought — THOUGHT — I could trust.

Pete Landry. His face was white. His hand trembled. "Jordyn? What are you doing—"

Before he could say anything else, I growled, lunged, and

grabbed his shirt collar with both hands. I wanted to yell at him, but there were so many words fighting to get out of my mouth, so instead of saying something coherent, I angrily shouted a strange mixture of consonants. But I shouted them directly into his face, which frightened him even more.

"Jordyn. Stop." Dylan peeled my fingers off of Pete. We were in his house, now. Standing in the foyer. In my rage, I'd driven him back against the wall, almost knocking a painting to the floor.

"You want me to stop?" I growled.

"Pushing him won't fix anything," Dylan said. He glared at Pete. "Kick him in the groin. It'll do more damage."

Pete simultaneously covered himself and tried to run away. Instead of succeeding at either, he awkwardly stumbled, tripped over his own two feet, and face planted on the floor. "I'm sorry," he said. "I'm sorry. I didn't mean to."

"You didn't mean to?" I wanted so badly to kick him, but he looked so pathetic curled up on the floor that I couldn't bring myself to do it. "You didn't MEAN to? So, you accidentally followed me? You accidentally took pictures? You accidentally sent them to Click? Click was after me because of your stupid accidents? Freaking hilarious. Why? Why would you do something like that? Tell me."

Pete was still covering himself. Problem was, now he also had tears in his eyes — tears he was desperately trying to wipe away. It was difficult for him to do both things at once. "I was trying to help you."

Help me? How on earth would anything involving Click possibly help me?

"When we were together—"

"We were never together," I yelled, sounding slightly hysterical. I took a quick step towards Pete and he whimpered again. UGH. Why did he do this?

"When we were... you always complained. You

complained that you were in Chase's shadow. So I thought...
maybe through Click... like Hailey helped Trey through
Click. I thought, maybe if I showed Click everything about
you, everyone would see you for who you are. Please don't
hurt me." Pete looked to me, then to Dylan, then back to me.
"I did everything for you."

"You did a bunch of things I never asked you to do," I said.
I could almost, ALMOST, understand his twisted logic. In
Evermore, Click turned people into stars, whether or not
they wanted it. If he made me popular on Click, I'd become a
star. If I was a star, people would stop referring to me as the
quarterback's sister. He was trying to give me a name.

But he was doing it in the worst way possible.

And he didn't understand why I hated being in Chase's
shadow to begin with. It wasn't because I wanted everyone to
know who I was instead of Chase. It was because I wanted to
earn things on my own. I'd rather be hated for who I was
than liked because I was the sister of the quarterback. But
bringing Click into everything? That didn't fix the problem.
If I was Click famous, I'd just be liked because of the rumors.

I just wanted someone to like me for me. To treat me as
an individual, and not as Chase Jones's sister.

"But, but, but..." Pete whimpered. "I wasn't wrong, was I?
You're dating Dylan?"

Pete didn't get it. At all. But before I could tell him as
much, Dylan spoke.

"Don't be an idiot," Dylan said. "We're not dating. Jordyn
and I are just friends. And that's all we ever will be. You
know the code."

Pete rubbed the tears from his eyes. "The code?"

"You don't date your best friend's sister. The code."

I flinched. There it was again. I wasn't Jordyn Jones, the
girl he liked. I was his best friend's sister. Was that all I'd ever
be to Dylan? To the world? Look at me, Jordyn Jones, the

sister of someone more popular. If Chase ever made the NFL, it would be a nightmare. The sister of an NFL quarterback. The ultimate cheerleader and supporting player.

*It's time to face facts, Jordyn. The most interesting thing about you is your brother.*

Heat creeped to my cheeks, and my eyes stung. I gripped my fists so hard that my fingernails left half-moons in my palm. If I worked quickly, I could redirect the hurt into anger. Or at least I could pretend that's what it was. Instead of saying something, I just shook my head and left, opting to stand outside near the car with my arms crossed.

A minute later, Dylan was beside me. "I told him to delete everything he has," Dylan said. "And to leave you alone. If anyone puts you on Click anonymously, I told him I'd assume it was him. And then he'd have me and Chase to deal with."

"Great," I said without enthusiasm. I got in the car. Apparently, even the solution to my problems was to use my brother's name.

## 42

# JORDYN

*M*usic blared through my headphones. A guitar riff, crashing cymbals, and a screeching singer came together to make the perfect theme song for what I was feeling: anger and pain. My Click nightmare was over, but another nightmare was just about to start. Chase would be home in two days.

Which meant that, in two days, Dylan and I were done. Or maybe, if I bothered to look at the evidence, we already were done. Our fake date was tremendously awkward. At Beachbreak, we only talked about work. And outside of work, we didn't send each other a single text.

I stood and paced through the dirty laundry laying on my floor. If our encounter with Pete proved anything, it was that no matter what I did, Dylan would always see me as Chase's sister. Even if he wanted to see me as Jordyn — and I thought he did — he couldn't do it. Which meant that even when Chase came back, we couldn't be together.

Ugh. If only I had someone to talk to.

I scrolled through the contacts on my phone. Hailey was still out of town. I could shoot her a text, but it wasn't the same. I wanted someone I could meet in person. Someone I could sit across from and reach out and touch. The ironic thing was, in the past, if I couldn't talk to Chase or Hailey, I always had Dylan.

Now… not so much.

I highlighted a name and sent a text.

A few hours later I was sitting in Peak's Frozen Yogurt. Peak's was THE place to go if you were looking to cool down on a hot summer day. The shop smelled of sugar and cotton candy, the frozen yogurt machines hummed in the back. Families and friends bustled through, each trying different mixes of flavors with different toppings.

Abby entered, her notebook curled under her arm. I waved her down. She eyed my frozen yogurt — a mix of Blue Raspberry and Vanishing Vanilla, topped with bright blue dolphin gummies and blue and white sprinkles — then set her notebook down.

"Be right back," she said, before whipping away to get her own frozen yogurt. She crafted a mixture of Birthday Cake and Decadent Chocolate, and topped it with peanut butter crunch, then returned. "I haven't seen you all summer. How've you been?"

That was a tough question to answer.

"Good," I said, feeling anything but good. "Busy. I've been working at Beachbreak for most of the summer. Haven't had time for much else. You?"

Abby tapped her notebook. "Internship at the Evermore Times. Lots of running around, scheduling interviews, double-checking facts. I've worked on a few columns, I'm hoping to get something off the ground by the end of summer."

Abby was one of those rare girls that seemed to have everything figured out. She was a talented writer, was likely to become the lead editor of the school paper in the fall, and already knew which college she wanted to go to. She knew what she wanted to do with the next five years of her life; I didn't know what I wanted to do with the next five minutes of mine.

She took a bite of her frozen yogurt, closing her eyes and savoring the taste. "This is the first place I actually talked to Chase. The first place we had a real conversation. Did he ever tell you I almost ran him over?"

"He might have mentioned it," I said. He did more than mention it. Whenever he told the story of how he and Abby met, her driving got more and more extreme. By now, when he told the story, Abby sounded like Cruella de Vil, swerving through Evermore like a maniac. I'll admit — I was jealous. From the way Abby and Chase talked about each other — and the way they wouldn't stop eating each other's faces — it was obvious how in love they were.

Maybe it was easy for them. Abby didn't have to worry that Chase was Jordyn's brother. It made no difference.

That's all I wanted.

"So, what's up?" Abby asked.

I didn't know where to start. "You know Dylan?"

Abby raised her eyebrows. "Are the rumors on Click true? I told Chase they weren't."

Ugh. That made it worse.

"This needs to stay between us," I said. "You can't tell anyone. Especially Chase."

"I won't lie to him." Abby's eyes narrowed.

"I don't need you to lie," I replied. "Just don't bring it up."

Her expression hardened, simultaneously making me proud that she was Chase's girlfriend, and annoyed that she wouldn't make an exception for me.

"I want to tell him," I said. "And I will. But… just give me a chance to get the timing right. Please."

She must have noticed the desperation in my voice,

because after a moment of hesitation, she nodded. "Tell me everything."

And so I did. I told her how Dylan and I started spending time together outside of Beachbreak. How he was the person I called whenever I needed someone to talk to. About the Ramirez Slip 'n Slide and our own Jones Family Drive-in. I told her about Click's pursuit of my secrets, and how Pete was behind it all.

"And… now Chase is coming back," I said. "So it has to end."

Abby looked confused. "Why?"

"Because."

Abby gave me the same look she gave a subject she was interviewing. A subject she suspected was hiding something. "Because why?"

I threw my hands up, feeling hopeless. "Because Dylan still sees me as Chase's sister. I'm not just Jordyn to him, not when Chase is around, or when anyone else is, for that matter. I want someone who will see me as more than that."

"Hmm."

Hmm?

Abby shook her head slowly. "There's something you're not telling me."

"But that's everything," I said. Was I holding something back? Was there some other reason why I felt things couldn't work out with Dylan?

*You know there is, Jordyn.*

I took a deep breath. "And you've met my parents. You've seen who they pretend to be… but you also know who they are. A long time ago, they were best friends. But look at them now. That's what love does to a friendship. It ruins it. And… I'm afraid if I let myself fall for Dylan, it's just going to ruin what we have." I looked at her hopefully. "Isn't it?"

Abby finished her frozen yogurt. She licked the spoon,

then set it back in the bowl. It was almost annoying — I probably looked like a total slob when I ate frozen yogurt; she somehow still looked intelligent. Thoughtful.

"I wish I had an answer for you," Abby said. "But there aren't answers. Not with love. There will always be a risk. You'll always have to put something on the line. And there's always the chance everything can go all wrong. You just have to decide what you're willing to risk, and when to risk it." She took my hand. "I'm sorry if I'm not more help."

"It's okay." I looked at my yogurt cup. It was empty. I couldn't remember eating it, couldn't remember enjoying it. If it weren't for the few streaks of blue at the bottom of the cup, I wouldn't have been sure that I had yogurt at all.

Abby was right.

With love, there was risk.

Love with Dylan might risk losing him forever.

And I didn't think I could take that risk.

## 43

## DYLAN

"*I*f you stare at those any longer, they're going to get cold," Luis said.

He was right.

I stood in the kitchen at Beachbreak eyeing three burgers. We had a double cheeseburger, garden style, a single cheeseburger, Cajun style, and a Midnight Meal. These were the burgers we'd be presenting to Christopher Lyons and his movie crew a week from now. If they liked the food, Beachbreak would win the contract to help cater the movie.

It was all I could think about. When I fell asleep, I had dreams about burgers. Actually, they were more like nightmares. I imagined all the things that could go wrong. I imagined giving one of the biggest movie directors on the planet an undercooked burger. I imagined him getting food poisoning, and Beachbreak being put on blast in the national media. Then a health inspection would come and—

"You okay?" Luis asked, drawing me from my anxious thoughts.

"I'm good."

"You look pale."

"I'm good," I repeated. Truthfully, burgers weren't the only thing on my mind. Since our encounter with Pete, things hadn't been going well with Jordyn. We only talked at work. Neither of us texted the other. And Chase was coming back soon. She was slipping away from me, and there was nothing I could do to stop it. Our fling had always been fragile, and now that reality surrounded us, everything was crumbling.

Luis patted me on the back. "Just nerves. You'll pull it together. You're good at this." He paused. "How's Jordyn? She called in sick."

"I don't know."

"I thought you were close."

I shrugged. "Close as any friends."

Luis snorted and rolled his eyes. "You were closer than that, from what I've seen."

I winced. It sucked to deal with relationship problems. But it sucked even more when you were dealing with relationship problems and everyone knew about it. My brother wasn't stupid, and neither was Sofia. I was sure they both figured out what was going on. But, so far, they'd both been too polite to say anything.

I sighed. "It's complicated."

"You're seventeen. How complicated could it be?"

"It just is."

Luis grabbed the next order slip, read it, and threw two fresh patties on the grill. They sizzled. "You like her. She likes you. You get together. That's how it works."

"Not with Jordyn," I said.

"Why not?"

"Because of who she is. And because of who I am." I pulled a basket of fries out of the deep fryer, shook them onto a tray, then scooped them into a basket. "We both agreed that when Chase got back, whatever we were doing stopped. Because she's not supposed to date his best friend, and I'm not supposed to date his sister. He's back this weekend, so things are…"

I didn't have the heart to say that things were ending.

"Is that what you want?" Luis asked.

"It's what Jordyn wants," I said. "And when Chase finds out, he's going to be mad. And I'll have to deal with that too."

"Have you talked to her about it?"

Frustration built inside of me. "Would you just let it go?"

Luis chuckled and flipped the burgers. He peeled plastic off two slices of cheese and set them on top. "All I'm saying is that you should talk to your girl before you jump to anything."

"She's not my girl," I said. And she never would be. Never could be. Jordyn never wanted to be with me in the real world. She was the one who wanted this to be a secret, to be a summer thing, separate from reality. And I was the one who'd let my heart get in the way of that.

I understood why Luis wanted me to talk to Jordyn. To figure things out. But it felt like things had already been decided, whether or not I liked it. And talking to her? That would only lead to an official breakup.

It was easier to live in denial than deal with the consequences of reality.

## 44

# JORDYN

*I* sat at the kitchen table and crunched down a third bowl of cereal. While I was eating, my parents came into the kitchen in turns. Dad first. He fished some leftovers out of the fridge without saying a word. Instead, he just stared at his phone the entire time, not meeting my eye. Mom came in next. She gave me a sad look, but also said nothing.

Not that I bothered to say anything to them. They were probably waiting for Chase to get back before talking to either of us about their impending divorce. Or they were just treating me like I was invisible, as per usual. If I wasn't actively causing problems, I wasn't seen.

Once mom left the kitchen, I finished my cereal and put the bowl in the sink. I didn't have time to worry about my parents' relationship; I was too busy dealing with my own problems. Dylan was on his way over. We were going to have a Talk, capital-T. About our relationship. About where it might be heading.

About how it might be ending.

It was what I had wanted, right? Dylan never fell for

anyone, he kept things casual with every girl he dated, so I had dictated our terms from the start. The rules were meant to keep my heart safe: it was a secret thing, one summer only. No feelings involved.

Except there were.

Mine.

I was the idiot who had fallen for Dylan Ramirez.

The doorbell rang and nerves shot through my body.

I walked to the door as slowly as possible. Each step was one step closer to the chopping block. The sooner I answered the door, the sooner everything would end. My heart was already fractured. It wouldn't take much for it to break.

I took a deep breath and opened the door.

Dylan smiled. There were dark circles under his eyes and creases on his face that reminded me of his father. As soon as he was inside, he wrapped his arms around me in a hug. I thought about resisting, but couldn't. I was sad, hurt, angry, and the worst part was that the only thing I wanted to fix those feelings was the one thing I was about to lose forever — Dylan himself. So instead of pushing back, I gave in, just for a moment, and circled my arms around him, pulling him tight against me, my hands balled up in the back of his t-shirt. I rested my head on his chest, inhaling his scent, and resisted the urge to cry my heart out.

We held each other for far too long to be 'just friends.'

Finally, I pulled away, took his hand, and led him to the kitchen. We sat at opposite ends of the table, like two lawyers ready to negotiate a contract. Or a divorce.

I broke the ice. "What are you thinking?"

He sighed heavily. "I'm thinking—"

Before he could finish, I heard the front door swing open.

Dad?

"Guess who's back! Anyone home?"

It was Chase.

Dylan and I exchanged panicked glances. What were we supposed to do? What were we supposed to say? Chase was home early, and by getting home early, he'd ruined our last chance to figure out our relationship.

Chase entered the kitchen, a big smile on his tanned face. When he saw Dylan and I sitting across from the table, his smile faltered, replaced by a look of suspicion. His gaze zeroed in on my puffy eyes. "Didn't realize we had company."

"It's just Dylan," I said, standing. I ran over and gave Chase a quick hug. "He barely counts as company. I'm glad you're home — now I have someone to take him off my hands. Hailey's supposed to be back soon, so I was going to run over to her place and hang out."

It was an absolute lie, and if Chase looked into it, it would be very easy to uncover. But I wasn't ready to face my brother, not yet.

So instead, I grabbed my jacket and disappeared, leaving Dylan to fend for himself.

I wasn't sure if that was a good idea, either.

## 45

# DYLAN

hase got back early from football camp, interrupting any chance I had to discuss my relationship with Jordyn. Instead, I spent the rest of the afternoon hanging out with Chase and hearing about what he'd learned at camp. For six weeks, he'd had his time split evenly between reviewing game film (with an emphasis on reading different coverages and blitzes), individual drills, and seven on seven scrimmages. During camp, a dozen college scouts watched from the stands.

Normally, I would've been happy to talk about football, and just football, for weeks. But I couldn't get Jordyn out of my mind. Was this how we were going to leave things? Everything felt unfinished, like we were reading a book only to find the ending missing. When Chase asked about Lauren, I laughed it off with a shrug. When he asked about Jordyn, I told him she was doing well at Beachbreak, but nothing beyond that. The guilt in my stomach was a balloon, inflating with each lie I breathed into existence. It would have to pop sometime. And it would be ugly.

The rest of my week was packed with shifts at Beachbreak. Unfortunately, none of them overlapped with Jordyn, so I never got the chance to even see her, much less talk to her. Aside from a handful of texts, it was the longest we'd gone without talking to each other all summer.

Friday morning, I had just finished packing my clothes when a car honked outside. I grabbed my bag and headed out the front door. Chase and Jordyn were waiting in a car in the driveway. Our annual end of summer trip to the Jones's mountain cabin. This trip was tradition for us and all of our friends, including Hailey, Trey, and Abby.

When we were younger, Chase and Jordyn's parents had taken us. This year would be the first year we were unchaperoned. I should have been looking forward to it, but I was filled with dread. I considered lying my way out of it, but I'd created enough lies to keep track of already.

I hated lying. Hated doing this to my best friend.

But I had to, for Jordyn.

I hopped in the backseat. "What's up."

Chase said nothing. Didn't even acknowledge me. Instead, he shifted into reverse, backed out of my driveway, then navigated through the neighborhood on the way to the interstate. Jordyn didn't say anything, either.

As long as I could remember, there had never been tension between the three of us. Never.

Chase sighed. "So. I think I need to ask you guys a question."

## 46

# JORDYN

*O*h no.

It was happening. All of my nightmares were coming together for this singular moment. The bubble Dylan and I had been living in was about to pop, and Chase's question was the pin that would pop it.

Chase steadied himself. His fingers were white on the steering wheel, his forearms tense. He licked his lips. "There's a lot of talk on Click about you two. I just want to know right now — is it true?"

What was I supposed to say? What was actually true? I didn't know. We hadn't had a chance to figure out our relationship. To figure out what we were. Not only did I not know what was true, I didn't even know what I wanted to be true.

Like a coward, I stayed quiet and internally pleaded for Dylan to bail me out.

Dylan was silent for a long moment, then cleared his throat. "It's all made up, dude. You know Click. We were just out doing regular things and people were trying to start some drama."

We passed a car.

"Good," Chase said. "Some of those photos were pretty convincing. But it's Click. Can't trust it. That's why I thought I'd ask."

"Don't worry about it, dude," Dylan said. "There is not now, nor will there ever be, something between me and your sister. Right, Jones?"

He sounded so, so confident. Not now. Not ever. Maybe that was the truth I was avoiding. The one thing I didn't want to confront.

If nothing was ever going to happen, it was for the best, wasn't it? Love destroyed everything. It had already done a lot of damage to our friendship. Dylan was just trying to save us.

So why did it hurt so much?

"Looks like you got something right for once, Ramirez," I snapped. Better to sound angry than to sound sad. Better to be feared than pitied. I connected my phone to the stereo, put on my road trip playlist, and cranked the music.

We were about halfway through the tunes when Chase pulled off the highway to get gas. He went inside to pay, leaving Dylan and I alone for the first time in forever.

There were a thousand things I wanted to say, but all the words felt wrong in my mouth. Once again, I took the coward's way out and stayed quiet.

"So, is it over?" Dylan asked. His voice was soft as November snow.

"That was the deal we made," I said. "Chase comes back, we go back to normal."

There was a long silence between us. I couldn't even remember what normal was supposed to look like. When you broke up with a friend, did you get to stay friends? Or was everything broken forever?

"Back to normal," Dylan whispered.

Chase emerged from the gas station and jogged back to the car. He frowned. "What's the matter with you two? Didn't get much sleep? Come on. This weekend is always the best part of summer."

It used to be.

But Dylan had been the best part of summer. The sarcastic comments and stolen kisses at Beachbreak. The Slip 'n Slide. The carnival Love Doctor that matched us together. Everything that I loved about this summer revolved around Dylan.

Sadly, summer was over.

## JORDYN

*I* laid on the bottom bunk bed while Hailey snored softly above me. I tried rolling over, tried flipping my pillow to the cool side, counting sheep, and about a hundred other things that were supposed to put me to sleep, but nothing worked. There was a storm inside my head, and every time I felt close to drifting off, there'd be another crack of lightning and rumble of thunder to keep me awake.

How could such a quiet breakup be so loud?

We arrived at the cabin late at night. Hailey, Trey, and Abby arrived shortly after. They had carpooled up in Trey's rickety van after Abby and Trey finished work for the day. I was over the moon to see my best friend, but I couldn't shake the sadness welling inside me as the evening went on. We sat around the table, played cards, ate snacks, and told stories about our summers. Not the full story, obviously. For most of the night, I was sitting right next to Dylan. But I couldn't do anything. Couldn't punch him in the shoulder. Couldn't reach out and touch him. Something that used to be so natural was now gone, ruined.

I was surrounded by people I loved, but I felt completely alone.

I sighed in the darkness and rubbed my eyes. If I wasn't going to get any sleep, there was no point in lying here and listening to my best friend snore the night away. I slipped out from under the covers, changed into my bikini, and exited, closing the bedroom door softly behind me.

Our cabin was in the mountains outside of Denver, up near Howls Lake. Mom and Dad bought the cabin when they found out she was pregnant, and it had been in our family ever since. So many of my earliest childhood memories, my favorite memories, took place on this mountain. Hiking with Chase. Trying to push Chase down a hill. Swimming with Dylan. Trying — in vain — to dunk his head beneath the water. The three of us, walking along the gravel road that led to the tiny village with the adorable ice cream shop.

I slowly crept through the darkness of the cabin, pausing to look at the framed photos. Summer memories, mom called them. There were so, so many of them. And unlike the photos that hung on our walls at home, these were actually happy. The smiles — mine, Chase's, Mom's, Dad's, and Dylan's — were real.

My chest hurt and my eyes stung. I was a ghost walking through scattered memories. Now I couldn't even think about all the time I spent with Dylan, even before we were dating, without hurting. Apparently, it only took a handful of dates to ruin my childhood memories.

I stole a towel from the bathroom, wrapped it around my waist, then slipped outside. Even in August, the mountain air was cool against my skin. The stars were bright and there was no moon. My teeth chattered slightly as I picked my way along the rock path. It was thirty feet long and wound through a cluster of pine trees. At the end of the path was a covered hot tub.

At least, it was supposed to be covered.

But, to my surprise, the cover was leaning against a tree and someone was sitting in the hot tub.

My heart stopped.

Dylan.

His eyes were closed, his head leaning back. He looked comfortable. Relaxed. I briefly debated whether or not I should bother him. He must have been having trouble sleeping too.

I chickened out. I turned to leave, accidentally stepping on a branch.

It snapped.

Dylan's head jolted up. He saw me and his expression softened. "Jones."

"Hey," I said, my voice barely carrying over the jets. "I couldn't sleep, so I was... it's okay, I'll just go inside."

Dylan shook his head. "It's all good. You can come in. Or I can get out. I've been out here for a while now, anyway."

"You can stay. We're supposed to still be friends, right?"

"Right." I hated how uncertain he sounded.

I took off my towel and hung it from a tree branch. I climbed the stairs, then slowly lowered myself into the hot tub. Hot water bubbled around me, massaged my body, and melted the tension from my muscles and my mind. I stretched my legs, accidentally hitting Dylan with my foot. "Sorry," I said quickly.

"It's okay." As he spoke, he shifted so he was on the exact opposite side of the hot tub.

For a long while, neither of us said anything. There was just too much we needed to talk about, too much to put into words. This time, I broke the silence.

"How've you been?" I asked.

Dylan ran his fingers through his hair and sighed. "Honestly, I've been better, Jones."

I wanted to swim across the hot tub. To take him in my arms and tell him everything would be okay. To kiss him. But instead, I anchored myself to the side, where it was safe. There was no need to make this more complicated than it already was. "Me too."

Dylan rested his head on the hot tub, staring up at the stars. "What are you doing tomorrow?"

"Hailey, Trey and I are going to check out the shops and have a picnic by the lake. You?"

"Chase and Abby want to go hiking. I'll probably tag along. Maybe throw the ball around later."

"Cool."

Ugh. It felt like trying to make conversation with someone I'd just met for the first time instead of someone I'd known my entire life. There were so many questions I wanted to ask him, but it was so hard to spit the words out of my mouth. Was he feeling the same way? Why was it suddenly so hard to talk to him now?

*You know why. Because love ruins everything.*

It did.

I knew with more certainty than ever in my life that it did. Two people could like each other, but as soon as they fell in love, their relationship was destroyed.

Just like mom and dad.

And now me and Dylan.

*You never learn, Jordyn.*

I felt another pain in my chest. I needed to get out of here. Now. No one got to see me cry. I couldn't be cool, unshakable Jordyn if I cried.

I faked a yawn. "Time for bed. Good night."

Before Dylan could protest, before he could even say good night, I was up and out of the hot tub.

I'd ruined our friendship.

I'd ruined my everything.

## DYLAN

*J*ordyn splashed out of the hot tub, grabbed her towel, and dashed into the darkness before I even realized what was happening. I put my head in my hands. I didn't blame her for running off. Not when I'd been so awkward. I didn't know what I was supposed to say. What I was allowed to say. Over the past few weeks, we'd destroyed the lines between a friendship and a relationship, and now we were awkwardly trying to re-establish them with disastrous results.

A cool mountain breeze rustled through the trees.

Alone once more, I stared at the stars. Jordyn had looked sad the whole day. Gone was our playful banter, the subtle jabs, the sly winks. But somehow worse than that, it felt like her competitive fire had been extinguished. Her competitiveness made her Jordyn, and the end of our relationship had snuffed out that flame.

"Get it together," I muttered to myself. She was the most amazing person I'd ever met. She was strong. She would bounce back. And as much as I wanted to find her, to hold her, to tell her how incredible she was, I knew I couldn't cross that line. Not again. Not when it had almost destroyed our friendship.

I climbed out of the hot tub, put the cover back on, then went to bed. My night was sleepless; no matter how much I tossed and turned, the only thing that changed was the red numbers on the alarm clock. Was Jordyn sleeping? Or had I ruined her night, too?

At some point, I must have fallen asleep, because I woke to the sun on my face. It was past ten and I could smell bacon and fresh coffee. I put on a pair of jeans and a t-shirt, slapped on some deodorant, quickly brushed my teeth, then went downstairs to the kitchen.

Chase stood over the stove, a spatula in hand, scrambling eggs and poking at bacon. Abby was sitting on the counter next to the toaster, diligently putting bread in, toasting it, then buttering it and setting it on a plate. There was a jug of orange juice next to her.

"Morning." I poured myself a glass. "How'd you sleep?"

Chase looked at me, frowning. "Never mind me, dude, you look like you got no sleep at all. You've got dark circles under your eyes and everything."

"Too wired," I said. "What's the plan for today?"

"We were thinking of doing a hike. But we're pretty flexible now that it's just the three of us."

My stomach dropped. "Just the three of us?"

Abby nodded. "Hailey wasn't feeling great, so Trey and Jordyn took her home. They think it's some kind of stomach bug. Apparently, she was up all night." Abby looked at Chase. "Which is weird. My room's right beside the bathroom, but I didn't hear a thing."

Chase shrugged. "Didn't hear anything from the couch, either. I was pretty tired from driving though. You hear anything?"

"No," I said. I didn't hear anything because there was

nothing to hear. It was obvious. Hailey's sickness was just a cover so Jordyn could leave without Chase asking her too many questions. I leaned against the counter and rubbed my eyes. Even the smell of bacon and coffee couldn't cheer me up this morning.

Jordyn left.

Things had gotten so bad between us that she actually left.

Was last night the last time we'd see each other as friends?

Or was that over too?

## 49

## JORDYN

*T*rees blurred outside the van window as Trey passed a silver Civic. An instrumental rock song played on the radio — one of Stonewash Sunrise's creations. Apparently, Trey liked to listen to it as he drove so he could try to think of lyrics that went with it. He kept his eyes on the road and paid no attention to what was going on in the backseat.

Hailey sat next to me, her tanned face practically glowing in the sun. Even with minimal makeup, she was still gorgeous. The kind of girl who made you do a double take when she walked in the room. But, more than that, she was the kind of girl who would do a favor for a friend without hesitation. Even if you didn't give her the full story.

And I definitely had not given her the full story. But that's what friends were for — they gave you their unconditional support. That was the friendship I had — or used to have — with Dylan.

Hailey smiled at me. "How're you feeling?"

I shrugged. My mouth was dry, and I had a headache. I

spent all summer looking forward to this weekend, then ran away before it really got started.

"You know you don't have to tell me if you don't want to," Hailey said. "But I'm here if you need me."

She'd never come out and say it, but she was dying to know why we'd left so suddenly. I was sure she had her suspicions, even if she'd never admit them.

I needed to tell someone. The more I kept my secrets to myself, the more they would eat me alive. And who better than Hailey? "I know you'll keep it quiet, but what about him?" I nodded to Trey.

Without answer, he turned up the music, his face a mask of concentration.

"Don't worry," Hailey said. "He'll stay in his own world if he knows what's good for him."

Trey smirked, nodded.

"Fine," I said. I lit the fuse, ready to drop the dynamite. "Dylan and I kissed."

Hailey's eyes widened. She kept her lips pressed shut, barely holding in a hundred thousand questions. I answered what I knew would be her most pressing question.

"We kissed a lot. All throughout summer."

Hailey screeched, her voice pitched so high that only dogs could hear it.

"Don't get too excited," I said. "It's over."

Her face fell. "Over? What do you mean, over? It's barely started."

"And there was a reason for that," I said. "Some things just aren't meant to be."

She rolled her eyes. "How are you possibly not meant to be? You've known each other forever. He was literally your first crush. You almost punched me because I didn't think he was cute."

"Almost? That doesn't sound like me."

"Maybe you did punch me. But whatever. How can it be over? Explain yourself, Jordyn Jones."

Ugh, where to start? I told Hailey how it all began. The competition at the carnival and the love doctor, flirting at Beachbreak, our first kiss at the Jones Family Drive-in. "And we agreed that because it was so complicated, when Chase got back, we'd end things. Because of the code or whatever."

Trey snorted.

I glared. "Got something to say, music man?"

"The code's a bunch of BS. If he really cared about some stupid code, he wouldn't have kissed you. But you do you." Trey skipped to the next track. This one opened with a guitar riff.

"Why would it matter if Chase was back?" Hailey asked.

"It just does."

"Why?"

"Because."

"Because why?" Hailey persisted, an annoying little smirk on her face.

"Oh my gosh, could you not?"

"Then tell me," Hailey said firmly.

"Because I'm Chase's sister. Because it's complicated. Because we were friends." I glared at Hailey, but to her credit, she didn't back down. "Because love ruins everything. Especially friendships. Not that that matters because I've probably destroyed things anyway."

I slumped in my seat. Ugh. UGH.

Hailey looked at me intently. "So. Do you love him?"

I stared out the window, hoping I could find something, anything, that I could use as a distraction to get me out of this conversation. But there was only trees, road signs, and mountains. None of which would be enough to get the bloodhound beside me off the scent of some juicy relationship drama.

"You love him," Hailey said. Not a question, a statement.

"Why do you think that?" I asked, feigning innocence.

"When I asked you if you and Pete were together, you gave me a hard denial. Every single time. You said no so many times I thought it was the only word you knew. But now, I ask you if you love Dylan, and you won't even deny it. Not once."

Ugh.

The worst part of having a best friend was that they knew you better than you knew yourself. And the worst part about what Hailey was saying?

She was right.

I was in love with my childhood friend.

I was in love with Dylan.

"It doesn't matter how I feel," I said.

Hailey rolled her eyes. Tapped Trey on the shoulder. "Mind pulling over?"

Trey signaled and pulled into a rest stop.

"Why are we stopped?" I asked.

Hailey smiled. She unbuckled her seat belt, opened the van door, and stepped out. A second later, there was a knock on my door. She was standing there, still smiling.

Had she lost her mind?

I slid open the door.

Hailey put her hands on my shoulders and looked me in the eye. "Jordyn. I love you. And I'm doing this for your own good."

Then she slapped me.

My cheek stung. Anger boiled through my veins. I lunged for Hailey, but the seat belt pulled tight, stopping my revenge and lightly choking me. "What was that for?" I growled.

"The first one is for being an idiot."

First one?

Before I could process what she said, she slapped me

185

again. Not hard. Not enough to do any damage, but enough to wake me up. Enough to make me angry. I reached to unbuckle my seatbelt while Trey chuckled from the driver's seat.

Hailey shoved me back down, then stepped away before I could swing at her. She knew me well.

"You sit down and listen, Jordyn Jones." Hailey had the tone of the meanest teacher in Evermore. "Falling in love with someone is rare. It's rarer than a shooting star. Rarer than a lightning strike. It does not happen every day. And for some people, it doesn't happen at all. Ever."

"What's your point?" I asked, gingerly rubbing my cheek.

"Falling in love with your childhood best friend and having a relationship? That's like seeing a shooting star get hit by lightning. If it works out, it's like winning the lottery."

"If it works out."

Hailey ignored me. "And you're sitting here, with the potential winning lottery ticket, and you're afraid to check it. Do you understand? You're willing to miss out on something amazing because you're afraid. And what are you even afraid of?"

"Have you met my parents?" I snapped. "Childhood friends. Got married. Now they hate each other."

Hailey was smart; she wouldn't deny the terrible marriage my parents were in. "So it didn't work. Sometimes relationships don't work. That's life, Jordyn. And I know you. I know you will keep pushing boys away if they get too close to you because you're afraid of ending up like your parents. And I get it, J. I do. Probably the only reason Dylan could get close to you was because he was your friend so you weren't paying attention. If you had been paying attention, you would've pushed him away too."

I grimaced and looked away, feeling the familiar sting in my eyes, the familiar heat in my cheeks. She was right. I pushed away every boy who actually liked me — or every boy I actually liked. In their place, I substituted weak, vanilla Pete Landry types. The type of guy who would never hurt me. And the reason they'd never hurt me? Because I'd never care enough about them to give them the chance.

Pete Landry could never hurt me. Not in a million years.

Dylan Ramirez? He could break my heart into a thousand pieces.

"So fine," Hailey said, still ranting. "Be an idiot. Be a coward. Push Dylan away. But if you keep pushing away the guys you care about, you will end up with Pete Landry. And what did you say about him? He had the personality of the color beige? If you keep being so careful, that's what you'll end up with. You won't be Jordyn Jones. You'll be Jordyn Beige."

I hated that she was right.

"So," Hailey said, raising her eyebrows. "What's it going to be? Are you going to take a chance, or do I need to slap you again?"

## 50

# DYLAN

*I* was the first one to the top of the mountain. My legs burned, and I was panting, but the view was worth it. Pine trees reached into the sky, a trail winding through them. The mountains gave way to rolling hills, and in the far distance, just on the edge of the horizon, I could see a small town. The view was so stunning that, for at least a moment, I forgot about all the drama in my life.

Chase and Abby followed close behind. Abby pulled out her phone and immediately started taking pictures, walking back and forth across the vantage point, searching for the perfect angle. She dipped back into the bushes, and Chase and I were alone on top of the mountain.

If there was ever a time to tell him about me and Jordyn, this was it. It was time to man up and admit the truth. No more lying.

"I got something to tell you," I said.

Chase stood beside me. We both stared at the horizon, our arms crossed, the morning sun on our faces. "What's that?" he asked.

There was no good way to tell your best friend that you

were seeing his sister over the summer. Especially when he thought you weren't interested in a real relationship. Would he think I was just using Jordyn? That we were just having fun? How would I make him see how much I cared about her?

"Jordyn and I got together over summer."

The words iced the air between us. Chase's fists clenched, but he remained composed. "And you told me this while we were standing on top of a mountain?"

"I was hoping you wouldn't throw me off."

"I'm still thinking about it," Chase grumbled.

"Let me know if I should start running," I joked. He didn't laugh.

"You lied."

"I did. And Chase, I'm so sorry. I didn't know what to do." I kicked at the ground. "We didn't mean for it to happen. I didn't mean for it to happen. It just... happened. It was unexpected."

Chase glanced at the bushes where Abby had disappeared. "I might understand that." His voice wasn't exactly friendly, but I didn't think he would throw me off the mountain. Which was a start, at least.

"I wanted you to hear it from me," I said. "And I wanted you to know that I care about her. A lot. It wasn't just some casual thing with a cheerleader. There was something real. Something that mattered."

"What a mess," Chase said. He rubbed his eyes. "I love Jordyn. And I'm protective over her. But, as much as I hate to say it, you don't need my permission. I know my sister. She's smart. Capable. And she makes her own decisions. If she got together with you for the summer, then that's cool."

It didn't sound like it was cool.

"Chase, I would never use Jordyn. I would never have gotten involved with her if I didn't have real feelings..."

"So, you're still together?" He cut me off.

I paused for a moment. "No."

"But you said—"

"She didn't want it to go beyond a summer thing."

Chase sighed. "You're going to need to give me some time. This is a lot to take in."

"I get it."

We stood in silence and watched the sun climb into the sky. Now and then, there was a rustling sound from the bushes as Abby scurried around to collect pictures.

"I'm sorry," I said.

"Don't apologize for falling in love with my sister," Chase replied. He turned to look at me — properly looking me in the eye for the first time in this entire conversation. "You do love her, don't you?"

I closed my eyes. "There's something I need to do."

## 51

## JORDYN

*W*e arrived home in the early evening, and I immediately retreated to my bedroom. I didn't feel like talking to anyone or dealing with anything. Besides, my parents probably barely noticed that I returned. It's not like I was Chase. What I did didn't matter.

I ate a tasteless bowl of cereal, then spent the rest of the night drifting in and out of a fitful sleep. Dreams of kissing Dylan mingled with nightmares of Chase and him fighting, Hailey slapping me senseless, Dylan telling me he didn't love me, didn't want me, that I was just another casual, meaningless thing to him. A summer fling to be forgotten.

A knock on my door woke me the next morning.

"What?" I asked grumpily.

The door creaked open. Chase. His face gave everything away immediately: he knew. Dylan must have told him everything. What had he said about me? What did Chase think? Was he ok? Was Dylan okay?

I opened my mouth to ask the first of a million questions, but Chase fixed me with a silencing glare. "Mom and dad. They want to talk to us."

"Great. Really looking forward to it." Chase didn't know what they would talk about, but I did. To say I wasn't looking forward to it was the understatement of the century. But, even if you knew you were about to be expelled, you still had to make the long walk to the principal's office.

In the living room, Mom and Dad sat next to each other on the couch, their hands folded together. Mom's eyes were puffy and Dad looked as tired as I'd ever seen him. The way they were sitting was like it was out of an after school special. It probably was, honestly. They probably spent all night watching cheesy TV shows to find the best way to break the news.

I sat on a chair in the corner of the room. Chase didn't sit, choosing instead to pace back and forth.

"We want you to know that we love you very much," Mom said.

I closed my eyes and waited for it all to end.

## 52

# DYLAN

Chase opened the door. His eyes were red, his smile was weak. He didn't look like the Chase Jones I knew. The confident, borderline cocky quarterback who called plays and threw touchdowns. He looked like a kid. Shy, sad. From the entry, I could see Abby sitting on the couch behind him, a box of tissues on her lap.

"Did she text you?" Chase asked.

"Yeah."

"Good," Chase said. "She didn't want to talk to me or Abby."

I stepped inside and closed the door behind me. "How are you holding up?"

"Rough," Chase said. "I knew the divorce was coming. It's been coming for a long time. But… it's still rough. Still…"

He couldn't finish his sentence.

I gave him a hug. Thumped him on the back. "If you need anything."

"Thanks, man."

He retreated to the couch and sat next to Abby. She

looked at me quizzically, then pointed to the bag I was carrying. "What's that?"

"They're for Jordyn." I set the bag on the table. "When she's ready. How is she?"

"She's in her room," Chase said.

"Okay." I left the bag on the table and went to Jordyn's room, gently knocking on the door. There was no response, but I didn't expect one. She hadn't officially told me what happened. All she did was text an emoji of a crying face. But that was all she needed to do to let me know that she needed me. I suspected her parents had officially announced their divorce, and Chase confirmed it.

I knocked again, then let myself in.

Jordyn was lying on the floor at the foot of her bed. She stared at the ceiling and didn't acknowledge my presence. It was like she was in a waking coma.

I closed the door quietly. Sat beside her on the floor and took her hand in mine. Her fingers were cold.

"I know it's a stupid question, but how are you?"

"You're right, Ramirez," Jordyn said. Her voice cracked. "It is a stupid question."

I squeezed her hand, then laid on the floor beside her, staring up at the ceiling.

We didn't talk for a long time. Sometimes, words weren't enough. I held her hand in mine, desperately wishing she would warm up. Despite the summer heat, it was strangely cold in her room. Like she was blasting the air conditioning.

As I laid there, I realized how important she was to me. Jordyn was a fixture in my life. If I thought back to a memory, there was a fifty percent chance it involved her. She was more consistent than the morning sun. Even though things didn't work out between us, if I ever needed her, she wouldn't hesitate. She would dig through the center of the planet to help me if I was on the other side. She was the girl who was always there for me.

And right now, she needed me to be there for her. Not as a boyfriend, but as a friend. She had way too much on her plate, way more than she should have to deal with, without worrying about our friendship. Sometimes, I decided, you have to sacrifice who you want to be for someone, for who they need you to be. And right now, Jordyn needed her friend.

"I love you, you know," I said. "You don't have to say anything. You don't have to do anything. You don't have to be anything. I can't imagine how hard this is for you. But I wanted you to know that I love you. And that through all of this, I'll always love you. And no matter what happens, we'll always be friends."

We laid there in silence for how long, I don't know.

Jordyn opened her mouth to speak. "We'll always be friends?"

Her voice sounded so quiet, so weak, so unlike the Jordyn I knew. It hurt to hear her this way, but I knew there was nothing I could do.

"Always," I said.

"Do you promise?"

"I promise."

"Thank you," Jordyn said. She coughed. "It's cold in here."

"Here." I stood, curled my arms underneath Jordyn, and lifted her off the floor. She wrapped her arms around my neck and nuzzled into my chest, then I laid her on the bed and covered her with the blanket.

"Don't go," she said.

"I won't." I laid on top of the blanket beside her. She put her arm around me and rested her head on my chest. My heart beat in sync with her breathing as we lay there in the shared silence you can only have with the people closest to you. I inhaled, committing every part of this moment to my memory. This could be the last time I would ever hold her. So I held on tight, and slowly but surely, we both drifted to sleep.

♥

SOMEONE KNOCKED ON THE DOOR. It was dark outside.

My arm was numb from the weight of Jordyn's head, but she was asleep. Finally. I closed my eyes again, not wanting reality to intrude.

There was another knock, then the door opened.

Chase stood in the doorway, back-lit by the hall light.

"Is she sleeping?" Chase whispered.

"Yeah."

"Good. Trapped?"

"Yeah."

He crossed the room. Carefully, so as not to disturb Jordyn, he lifted her head so I could pull out my arm. I gave her a soft kiss on the forehead, then exited.

Chase closed the door quietly, and we went to the kitchen. He poured us each a glass of water. "Abby had to go," he said. "Big assignment for the Evermore Times."

"Good for her."

"She's a smart girl." Chase finished his water and poured another glass. "How's Jordyn?"

"She's taking it hard," I said. "We didn't talk much. But I need to say something, because I owe you at least that much. No more lies. That wasn't cool."

Chase nodded.

"I want to tell you that you were right: I love her. I am completely and totally in love with her. So I told her. And then I told her that no matter what happened, we'd always be friends."

Chase looked confused. Or maybe he was just tired. "So are you—"

"No," I said quickly. "She doesn't need a boyfriend right now. She needs a friend. Someone she can trust without worrying that things will get screwed up. Someone who will love her unconditionally. I don't think she could handle a relationship right now, so I'm not going to push for one."

I knew it was the right thing to do for Jordyn, but it still hurt to say the words out loud. More than anything, I wanted to be with her. But she needed something else right now.

"I thought we'd have this big moment, just the two of us," I said. "A Ramirez special. I had it all played out in my head, that it would be this huge movie moment where the guy gets the girl and it's a perfect, happy ending… and then I saw her. And I just knew."

"You're a good friend," Chase said. He gave me a hug and patted me on the back. "Plus, maybe not being together is for the best right now. Let the dust settle on everything. But it ain't over yet. Maybe she'll come around at some point. Or maybe she won't. You know as well as I do — no one tells Jordyn what she's going to do or when."

I laughed quietly. "No one tells Jordyn anything."

Chase walked me to the door. "What about the bag?"

"Keep it," I said. "It was for Jordyn. Don't know if she'll want it or not. You can look and decide whether to give it to her. If the time is right."

I stepped out into the night. "Do you need anything?"

"We'll be okay." Chase clapped me on the shoulder. "You're a good friend, Ramirez. The best. And if it had worked out differently, I would've been happy to see you and Jordyn together."

## 53

# DYLAN

*I*t was the moment of truth.

Christopher Lyons, director of the next major superhero movie franchise, was seated alongside his producers, a location scout, and an intern. They booked Beachbreak's entire riverside patio for themselves for lunch. If they liked our food, we'd land the catering contract. If they didn't, we wouldn't.

Luis and I prepared the food, expertly crafting burgers, Cajun fries, and milkshakes. Nervous energy rolled through me in waves. One minute, I was excited. The next minute, I was tired. The minute after that, I wanted to throw up. Then I was excited again.

Everything my father had built depended on this meal. As crazy as it sounded, the burgers I made would determine whether Beachbreak could expand and launch new locations, or would remain a small mom and pop restaurant for the rest of its life.

I put the food on a tray and carried it out of the restaurant.

Dad was at the top of the stairs. He'd decided that the best thing to do was give the movie people their space. Let the food do the talking. He smiled at me. "Smells good."

"I hope it tastes as good as it smells," I said. My voice cracked.

Dad laughed. "I'm sure it's excellent. You're a Ramirez, after all. Good luck."

I walked down the stairs as carefully as I could. How would it look if my feet caught and I tripped, sprawling down the stairs, burgers and shakes spilling everywhere? Never in my life had I fallen down these particular stairs, but part of my mind was one hundred percent sure this was the time I would fall.

I made it to the bottom without causing a disaster and breathed a sigh of relief.

"And here's our meal, gents." Mr. Lyons stood, his wiry frame straightening to an imposing height. He reminded me a lot of the boy who'd been in here, chatting to Sofia — fair haired and blue eyed, with angular, aristocratic features, and a posh British accent. "Just in the middle of the table will be fine. We want to try everything you have."

"Thanks," I said. I didn't know what else to say. What could you say to the man who had directed superhero movies that made — literally — billions of dollars? I set the tray in the center of the table, and even before I left, people were scrambling to get their hands on their favorites.

Mr. Lyons laughed. "Stay a minute, this won't take long. I'm a firm believer that you can tell everything you need to know about food when you take the first bite."

The rest of the crew watched as Mr. Lyons grabbed the last burger and fries from the tray. I recognized it immediately — a Midnight Meal. One of my creations would decide the fate of my father's restaurant.

I put my hands behind my back and stood as straight and proud as I could. I tried to control my trembling legs. This was more nerve-wracking than the last minute of a playoff game.

My heart pounded in my chest.

Mr. Lyons lifted the burger to his mouth and took a bite. He closed his eyes, chewed the meat, tasted the flavor. Without a word, he reached for his napkin, then dabbed the corner of his mouth. He put the burger back on the plate. His eyes found me.

"That, young man, is one of the best burgers I've ever tasted."

I exhaled.

The rest of the crew dug into their burgers and it was more of the same. Plenty of compliments to go around. More than a few excited swears. Meanwhile, I was still standing in disbelief.

One of the best burgers he had ever tasted.

And it was something I'd created.

"Send your old man down," Mr. Lyons said. "I'd like to sign Beachbreak to handle part of the movie's catering. I think we could all do with a burger and fries once a week, agreed gents?"

Relief flooded through me.

My legs shook as I walked up the stairs. I needed to hold the railing to stop myself from falling over. We'd done it. We'd actually done it. Dad had been off most of the summer, and Luis and I had come together to help fulfill his dream.

We'd done it.

Dad and Luis waited at the top of the steps. Dad had his hands clasped tightly together. "Well?"

"They must have liked it," I said, "because they want you to go down there and sign to cater the movie."

Luis gasped, wobbled, and almost fainted.

Dad clasped my shoulders. "Are you joking? If you are joking, this is not funny, mijo."

I grinned. "Get down there, Dad."

Dad smiled the biggest smile since the day Sofia was born. "Come here. Both of you."

We did.

Dad put his arms around our shoulders, pulling us into a huddle. "You boys always make me proud, but today... I could not have been blessed with finer sons. You two, and Sofia, have outdone yourselves. We will throw a party for Beachbreak. A party to end all parties. No one does anything by themselves, so invite the people you love."

He kissed me and Luis on the forehead, clicked his heels together, then danced down the stairs.

Luis hugged me. "We did it, bro. We did it."

"Yeah, we did." I grinned and threw my arm over his shoulder. We watched from the top of the stairs as Dad approached the table, smiling and laughing. I thought about his words.

No one does anything by themselves, so invite the people you love.

There was one person I really wanted to share this moment with. I didn't know if she'd be up for a party, but she was the one I loved. I pulled out my phone and sent her a text. If it was anything like the other texts, there wouldn't be a response.

But I had to try.

## 54

## JORDYN

For supper, I ate yet another bowl of cereal. This time, I subbed out Froot Loops in favor of Cap'n Crunch. It was important to get your nutrition from a variety of different sources. I poured myself a glass of orange juice, because I was incapable of eating anything but breakfast food at the moment. Chase was at Abby's. He stopped by my room before leaving, asking if I would be okay. I said I would be.

And so I was alone.

Again.

There were footsteps on the stairs, and a moment later, mom entered the kitchen. Her puffy eyes were lined with dark circles. She dabbed at them with a tissue, then tried to smile. "How are you... are you eating cereal for supper? Again?"

"That answers your question, doesn't it?" I snapped. The last thing I could handle right now was being judged for my dietary habits.

"I'll make us some spaghetti. Top it with extra cheese, the

way you like." Mom's smile was pleading. She desperately wanted to do something, anything right. And making me food was the most motherly thing she could think of. It was also the most motherly thing I could remember her doing.

"Spaghetti sounds good." I pushed my cereal bowl to the side. My stomach grumbled in agreement. Apparently, it wasn't a fan of four bowls of cereal a day.

Mom found a pot, filled it with water, and put it on the burner. She added a dash of salt. "My mom used to say that the key to making great pasta was to make sure the water was as salty as the sea." She dipped her finger in the pot and licked it. Winced. "That should do it."

I sat very still. When mom buzzed around the kitchen, it usually meant she was building to something. A confrontation about something I did wrong. If she said anything about how I was handling the divorce, I was grabbing my bowl of cereal and locking myself in the bedroom.

The water boiled.

Mom broke a handful of spaghetti in half and set it in the pot, using a wooden spoon to force the pasta beneath the bubbling water. "Your dad and I want you to know that this divorce has nothing to do with you and Chase."

"That's a relief," I muttered.

Normally, my sarcasm drew withering glares.

Today, it made mom smile. "That's my girl," she said. "We love you both very much. And we know that we've treated you unfairly in the past. I can't speak for your father, but I know I've compared you to your brother. I've expected you to be like him, but you're not him. You're your own person, and you should be proud of that. I'm proud of you too, sweetie. You're different from Chase, and we should treat you differently. I want to do better at showing you that."

To say I was shocked would undersell what I felt.

Throughout my entire life, mom had never admitted that she expected me to be like Chase. Whenever I confronted her about it, she denied it. And now she was admitting it? Without prompting?

This wasn't a normal mother-daughter chat.

My phone vibrated. A text from Dylan wondering how I was and asking if I was going to Beachbreak's party. I was proud of him, proud of Beachbreak, but I wasn't sure I was up to seeing other people. I didn't reply.

"Come here," Mom said. "I want to show you something."

I went over.

"Do you know how to tell if pasta is cooked?"

"By biting it?"

"Nope. Like this." She plunged a fork into the boiling pot and pulled out a noodle. She grabbed the noodle, winked, and threw it onto the ceiling. It stuck.

My jaw dropped.

Mom.

My mom.

The woman who despised how messy my room was. Who despised how I kept my clean and dirty laundry in carefully separated piles on the floor. Who couldn't believe that I would wear a shirt with a stain on it. That same person had just thrown a piece of food on the ceiling.

"Do you want to try?"

I snatched the fork from her hand and scooped out a string of spaghetti. I looked at her once to reassure myself that it was okay, then I threw the pasta to the ceiling. It stuck for a breath, then peeled away and fell—

Into mom's hair.

Typical, Jordyn. You get the chance to do something fun with your mom and you screw it up.

But mom didn't frown. Didn't scream.

Instead, she burst out laughing as the string of spaghetti

dangled between her eyes. She crossed her eyes and stuck her tongue out as she tried to focus on it. And then I was laughing. We were both laughing too hard to trust ourselves with moving the pot of boiling pasta to the sink to strain it, and when we finally did, our spaghetti was delightfully overcooked.

"We're going to be okay, you know," Mom said as she set a plate of pasta on the table. "You, me, Chase, your dad. This divorce isn't the end of the story, just the end of the chapter."

We ate dinner together in the darkness of the kitchen, not bothering to turn on a light. There was a sadness between us, but there was something more, too. Something nice and whole and warm. It felt, at least for one night, that I was just a kid again, and my mom was a superhero.

"I know it's a crazy time in our lives, but do you want to do this weekly? Just you and me? We'll cook a meal together, or go out somewhere? Just us?" Mom asked.

I smiled. "I'd like that."

"Me too." Mom reached across the table and squeezed my hand.

The front door opened. Chase was back. He said hi, then rushed upstairs.

I finished my supper, cleaned my plate — probably for the first time in history — and went to my room. There was a bag resting on my unmade bed.

"Chase?"

Without waiting for a response, I started digging through the bag. There were two stacks of flash cards, each bundled together with an elastic. The cards were white with pink lining and little pink hearts on the back. They looked familiar.

I pulled the elastic off one and turned it over.

My handwriting was on the other side.

*I refuse to answer this question on account of it being stupid.*

The cards from the Love Doctor. I smirked and checked the other cards.

*I see another stupid question.*

*Samuel Danielson.*

*Samuel Danielson.*

If the first set of cards were mine, then the second set must have been…

I ripped the elastic off so fast it snapped. I recognized the handwriting immediately.

Dylan's.

My breath caught as I read his answers.

If the world tilted on its side, where would you land?

*Hopefully some place where I didn't have to answer this question.*

An animal spirit resides within us all. Tell me, what is the name of the animal that resides within you?

*Jordyn's stuffed animal.*

I snorted. What were the odds?

Then the last question.

When the clock strikes midnight, and there's nowhere to run, to whom do you turn?

I turned over the card.

*Jordyn Jones.*

I wanted to cry.

"Dylan left those for you." Chase leaned against the door frame. "We didn't stay at the cabin after you left. We drove to Kansas and caught up with the carnival. Found the Love Doctor — and her cards. Apparently — and this sounded stupid to me — if she thinks she finds an actual true match, she keeps the cards. Yours and Dylan's were the only ones she kept all summer. He wanted to give them to you. It was supposed to be his big moment."

I clutched the cards to my chest, still fighting off the urge to cry. "Typical Ramirez," I sniffed. "Still can't compete with me."

"You sound like you have something planned."

"Maybe," I said. "And if I did, it would definitely be better than what Ramirez came up with."

"It's not a competition."

I stood. "It's always a competition. And I'm going to win."

## DYLAN

*M*y foot was heavy on the gas as I cruised along the highway. Only two hours ago, I received a text from Jordyn. It was simple, small, and straight to the point.

Jordyn: Meet me where I had the best day of the summer.

Dylan: When?

Jordyn: Sunset.

I knew better than to ask where. There was only one place it could be.

I passed the sign for Evermore Lake. It was near sunset, and there were a few clouds in the sky. It had rained off and on throughout the day. As I took the turnoff towards the lake, my heart was beating in my chest so hard that I thought it would explode.

What did Jordyn want?

# JORDYN

*J* stood at the top of the hill and surveyed the water. It was raining lightly, just enough to cool me off after another hot summer day. The sun rested on the horizon, its brilliant orange rays turning the parts of the sky that weren't covered with clouds a beautiful pink. It was the same color as the lilies that Dylan bought me.

My heart was in my throat.

Was I doing this?

Was I actually doing this?

Tires crunched in the gravel parking lot. An engine turned off. A car door opened, closed. Footsteps approached.

I turned.

Dylan stopped. His mouth fell open as he took in the scene I had prepared.

I swallowed my fear. Grinned and cocked my eyebrows. "You said you wanted a big moment, Ramirez. How's this?"

## DYLAN

Was.

Speechless.

The Ramìrez Slip 'n Slide hugged the hill, rain droplets trickling down the plastic sheet. On either side of the slide, Jordyn had set up tea light candles, the fake ones with flickering LEDs. It was the second most amazing thing I'd seen in my life.

And the most amazing thing?

Jordyn.

She wasn't wearing anything special. No ball gown, no fancy sundress. Just her signature cut-off shorts and a tank top. Her hair fell over her shoulders, messy as usual. And she had that smirk. That competitive smile she always got before she was about to claim victory.

She looked 100% completely, uniquely Jordyn. Completely beautiful. Completely perfect — just the way she was.

Rain fell, just enough to wet the ground and the slide.

Jordyn glanced at the sky and smirked again.

This girl was so amazing she might have been able to control the weather, too. I wouldn't put it past her.

Finally, my voice returned. "How did you—"

"Sofia," Jordyn said.

She stuck out her hand, and I took it.

## JORDYN

*D*ylan's hand was warm. I opened my mouth, but the words I'd spent all afternoon preparing wouldn't come out. Now that Dylan was standing here, in front of me, it was terrifying. Even though I was ninety percent sure he felt the same way. Back when we were twelve, he was the first boy I had feelings for. I hadn't been able to tell him how I felt then.

And now?

Now, if I really thought about it, he was the only boy I had ever had feelings for. And I couldn't bring myself to spit out the words. To tell him how I felt.

Ugh.

Come on!

Say it, Jordyn.

"I love you."

But the words didn't come from me. They came from Dylan. And when they came, they knocked all thought and sense out of me. He continued. "I love you, Jordyn Jones. And I want to be with you. Forever. But if that's not what you want, and all I get is this summer, that's okay. Because dating you for one summer still makes me the luckiest man alive."

I gaped. How was I supposed to follow THAT? Even the pretty words I'd spent all afternoon preparing didn't compare to Dylan's off-the-cuff declaration of love. Even I, the most competitive person on the planet, couldn't compete with that.

"Slide?" I said, my voice weak.

"Slide."

I stripped down to my bathing suit and Dylan took off his t-shirt. He was already wearing his swim shorts.

I sat at the top of the slide and motioned for him to sit beside me.

He did.

I nudged him with my shoulder, and he turned, his wild eyes locking on mine. "I love you too, Dylan. More than anything. And I want to be with you. But if we're going to do this, we need to do it together. We need to be all-in. No matter what."

"No matter what." He whispered.

I stuck out my hand.

Dylan took it.

"On three?" I asked.

He nodded. "On three."

One.

Two.

Three.

We pushed off. Our fingers interlaced, we careened over the wet slide, huge smiles on our faces. As we went down the hill and crossed the beach, our smiles turned into wild, crazy laughter. We bumped into each other and skittered off the end of the slide.

Cool lake water enveloped us, and beneath the surface, we found each other.

We emerged from the lake like we had so many weeks ago, with my arms around his neck. I had just enough time to take a deep breath before Dylan pulled me in for a kiss. I felt the heat of his body against mine, and I felt the smile on his lips as they touched mine. Fireworks exploded across my skin as I wound my hands through his hair, pulling him closer, never wanting to let go.

I'd known Dylan my entire life. It was one of the best friendships I ever had. And, for the first time, I felt that we could truly be something more. Love didn't have to drive us apart. We were strong, and love would only make us stronger.

With Dylan Ramirez by my side, I could take on the world.

And win.

## 59

## JORDYN

*M*y heart beat furiously. Dylan and I hadn't told anyone what we were doing, or where we were. Or even that we were together. We took a few final days inside our bubble. Inside the place where it was just us, away from the scrutiny of Evermore and Click, holding a secret that joined our hearts. And now, a few days later, we were finally ready for the bubble to pop. It was the last weekend of summer, and Beachbreak's party to celebrate winning the catering contract for the movie was about to start.

I felt the warmth of Dylan's hand in mine. From Main Street, I could hear Stonewash Sunrise playing down by the river.

"You sure you're ready to make this official?" I asked Dylan.

"You better believe I am." He pulled me close and stole a kiss, then turned to the stairs. "Let's do this, Jones."

"Let's do this, Ramirez."

We climbed down the stairs. Everyone from Beachbreak was present. All the staff, all their family. Our closest friends were there too. Hailey was dancing with Chase and Abby in front of a small stage set up for Trey's band. Sofia bobbed her head to the music. My mom was there, too. She was sitting at a table near the back, watching the concert, a milkshake in hand.

Hailey was the first to see us.

Her eyes went to my face. Then to my hand, which was holding Dylan's.

She shrieked.

Then burst through the crowd and launched herself at the two of us.

"You finally got together!" Hailey squealed. "It only took, what, a decade?"

"Don't blame me," I said. "That's how long it took him to learn how to cook. And you know I won't date anyone that can't cook."

Hailey rolled her eyes. "Pfft. Until him, you wouldn't date anyone at all. Apparently you have to be friends with Jordyn Jones for sixteen years before she'll admit to being your girlfriend."

Dylan pulled me close. "She's worth the wait."

Hailey gagged. "I think my stomach turned. Is this how Trey and I sound?"

"You're way, way worse," I said.

Hailey released me, and was immediately replaced by Chase. My brother wrapped us both in a bear hug.

"It's about time," he said. "Way to let the suspense build over the last week."

"Just keeping you on your toes," I replied.

He grinned. "So? How do you feel?"

## 60

## DYLAN

*W*hen Chase asked us how we felt, only one word came to mind:

Lucky.

I was in love with Jordyn Jones. And she was in love with me. How else could I possibly feel? I squeezed her hand, and she squeezed back. We wandered into the crowd, skipping the food for now, and danced.

Trey stood at the microphone, smirking at us. "And this next one's for the happy couple."

Jordyn cupped her hands over her mouth. "This better have an awesome guitar riff, Trey, or I'll come up there and kick your—"

Trey smiled and ripped into his guitar before Jordyn finished her sentence.

Jordyn grinned at me.

I smiled back. "What do you say, Jones? Want to have a dance?"

Jordyn shook her head. "No, Ramirez. I don't want to have a dance. I want to have a dance-off. You against me."

"Is this how it's going to be for the rest of our lives?"

Jordyn barely held back a laugh. "The rest of our lives, hey?"

"I didn't mean—"

"You said forever. And combine that with the fertility flowers you gave me—"

"They weren't—"

She burst out laughing. "You're too easy."

I growled and playfully poked her in the side. "All right. You asked for it. We're having a dance-off. Game on, Jones."

She smiled. "Game on, Ramirez."

# JORDYN

*A*fter the party, the six of us sat by the river. Dylan was next to me, his toes submerged in the water, his arm around me. I rested my head on his shoulder. Abby sat in Chase's lap, and Trey was whistling while skipping stones across the river. Hailey lay on the beach like she was trying to top up her tan, even though it was nighttime.

Behind us, the Beachbreak Burgers riverside tables were empty for the first time this summer. Everything was cleaned and everyone had gone home.

"This was the first place I took Abby," Chase said. "Our first date."

"The cliché date," Abby said. She smiled. "You bought me chocolate roses."

"A dozen."

Abby snorted. "You don't get to say you brought me a dozen chocolate roses if you ate half of them first."

"I thought it was the thought that counted?"

"Chocolate counts more." Abby grinned and gave him a kiss. Mercifully, they did not start eating each other's faces.

Trey skipped a stone across the water. "This was where we had the concert that got Stonewash Sunrise into Prohibition. Right along the river."

"You're welcome," Hailey said in a sing-songy voice.

Trey dove onto the sand beside her. Tickled her until she shrieked.

Hailey jumped on top of him and pinned him down. "Say it, Trey Carter. You wouldn't be who you are if it weren't for me."

Trey smiled. "I confess. I would not."

They kissed.

Dylan spoke next. "And the raft you used for the concert, I used for our secret date. All of our relationships started near this river. Seems fitting that we should spend the last weekend before school starts here."

I patted his chest. "You know what else brought us all together?"

I waited for an answer, but no one raised their hand.

"Click," I said. "Chase and Abby wouldn't have got together if someone wasn't after Chase on Click. Hailey needed Click to get fans for Trey. And Dylan and I spent our entire summer trying to avoid being a Click rumor — before we dealt with Pete."

Dylan and Chase both grumbled.

I laughed. "Easy boys."

Dylan pulled me close.

It had been a crazy summer.

Scratch that — it had been a crazy year. Three relationships. Each sealed on the river, each started by Evermore's most notorious gossip app. While we had all found our happily ever afters, I couldn't help but wonder:

With the hallways of Evermore High on the horizon next week, would Click bring more couples together?

Or would its attempts at sabotaging people's lives win?

While our story was over, gossip lived forever.

Thank you so much for reading!

If you enjoyed this book, please leave me a review. As a new author, reviews mean everything to me. I appreciate each and every one of them.

Made in the USA
Coppell, TX
25 March 2022

75451775R00132